BLAZE

HOUNDS OF HELLFIRE MC

FIONA DAVENPORT

Copyright © 2024 by Fiona Davenport

Cover designed by Elle Christensen

Edited by Jenny Sims (Editing4Indies)

All rights reserved

No part of this book may be reproduced in any form or by any electronic or mechanical means, including information storage and retrieval systems, without written permission from the author, except for the use of brief quotations in a book review.

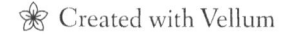

❊ Created with Vellum

BLAZE

Pax "Blaze" Driscoll was an expert on fires, but he never expected to fall for a woman in the middle of a flaming building. Especially not after she accidentally set fire to a Hounds of Hellfire MC warehouse.

Courtney Cartwright's roommate disappeared without a trace after she stole from the wrong people. They're out for blood...and Courtney is smack dab in their crosshairs. But Blaze will burn down the world before he lets anything happen to his woman.

1

COURTNEY

After logging out of my banking app, I set my phone on the coffee table with a sigh. Sabrina had really done a number on me when she disappeared out of nowhere a month ago, only a day before our rent was due. My roommate had been acting a little off in the days leading up to when I last saw her. I hadn't thought much about it because she'd never been the most dependable person.

Sabrina and I had been living together for almost two years, and in that time, she'd gone through six jobs and seven boyfriends. She'd been late with her half of the rent more often than not, but usually only by a few days. She'd always somehow pulled through in the end. Until now.

I didn't make a ton of money as a bank teller, but

I was good about setting some aside every paycheck. So I'd easily been able to cover her half last month. Doing it again would take my savings account lower than I liked, but I just transferred the funds because it wasn't as though I had a choice and had no way to contact Sabrina.

With that done, I stood and headed into the kitchen to make a mug of hot chocolate. The weather was warm for April, but I didn't care. Topped with a swirl of whipped cream that I had pre-frozen with a sprinkle of broken candy canes that I had left over from Christmas, it was my guilty pleasure. And with how bummed I was about the state of my bank account balance, I deserved something to cheer me up.

Unfortunately, the universe didn't agree.

Someone pounded on my door just as I took my first sip of chocolatey deliciousness. Setting my mug on the kitchen counter, I was not happy.

I wasn't expecting any visitors this morning, so whatever rude person thought it was okay to make so much noise this early in the day would get a piece of my mind. Only the words dried in my throat when I swung open the door and found three burly guys standing there.

Pressing my hand against my chest, I mumbled, "I think you've got the wrong apartment."

"No, we don't." The tall, lanky man who pushed between two of them was the only one I recognized.

I hadn't seen Sabrina's boyfriend since about a week before she disappeared. I'd hoped that meant she and Jason broke up, which I'd been secretly rooting for because he was even worse than all of her other bad boyfriends. That was saying a lot since she had awful taste in men.

I glared up at him. "If you're looking for Sabrina, she's not here."

"I know," he growled, bumping past me to walk into the apartment.

The other guys followed him inside, and I had no desire to be behind closed doors with any of them. I was in my pajamas without socks or shoes on, my phone was in the kitchen, and my purse was hanging on the wall about five feet away from me, but I seriously considered making a run for it. My thoughts must've shown on my face because the man closest to me wrapped his hand around my upper arm and yanked me away from the door so he could close it.

I tried to pull my arm free from his grip, but he only tightened his hold on me until I stopped fighting. Wincing in pain, I muttered, "What do you want, Jason?"

"What Sabrina stole from me."

My eyes widened as I gaped at him. My roommate was a lot of things, but I never would have thought she was the kind of person who'd rob someone, even a guy she was going to dump. "She took something from you? What?"

The biggest of the guys shot an angry look at Jason before answering my question. "Shit that belonged to our boss, not this idiot who shoulda known better than to mouth off to some chick."

The man holding my arm nodded. "Yeah, the bitch wouldn't have known there was anything to steal if you'd kept your trap shut."

"It wasn't my fault," Jason whined, his shoulders slumping. "I never thought Sabrina would do me dirty like that. I thought she loved me, man."

The third guy, who hadn't spoken yet, shook his head. "How in the hell are you still talking about that damn girl? I woulda thought the beatdown we gave you because of the shit she pulled would've knocked some sense into you."

My gaze darted toward Jason, and I finally noticed the split in his brow and the bruise forming on his jaw. I'd been so distracted by the men with him when they pushed their way inside my apartment that I'd missed it before. Knowing that he'd been beaten up over whatever Sabrina stole from him ratcheted up my fear several notches—which was saying a lot since I was already freaked all the way out.

About a million questions were running through my brain, but I didn't ask any of them. The last thing I wanted was to draw the men's attention to me while they were focused on Jason. Unfortunately, being quiet didn't prevent that from happening because he proved to be as big of a jerk as I thought he was.

Pointing at me, he cried, "I'm not the one who can help you find Sabrina, she is!"

The guy holding my arm finally let go, but only to line up with the other two directly across from me. The bigger one was in the middle, and he growled, "Where is she?"

"Sabrina?" I squeaked, shaking my head. "I don't know."

He jerked his thumb toward Jason. "That's not what he told us. Said you're the person who's closest to her, and the way we asked, he was highly motivated to tell the truth. So you're the only lead we got since we wasted the past four weeks tracking his pathetic ass down, only to find he doesn't have what the boss sent us looking for."

"And the guy we work for? We can't go back to him empty-handed," the grabby guy explained.

The third one nodded. "Which means *we're* highly motivated to get your friend's location outta you. The hard way or the easy way. The choice is up to you."

"Roommate," I whispered, my voice shaking.

The big guy's brows drew together. "What?"

"Sabrina isn't really my friend. She was my roommate, that's it," I explained with a wince, mentally kicking myself for correcting the description of who Sabrina was to me. Considering the current situation, it didn't really matter. They seemed desperate to find her, and Jason had tossed me to the wolves to save his own butt.

"I don't care if she's your sister, best friend, roommate, or mortal enemy." The big guy took a step closer. I moved back but bumped into the wall behind me, and his lips curved into a satisfied sneer. "You're gonna help us find her, or I'm gonna be forced to do something I don't enjoy—beat the shit out of a woman."

My gaze darted toward Jason, which made the guy who'd tugged on my arm laugh. "Don't worry, he'll get his ass kicked either way. Maybe worse, depending on if that bitch still has what she stole from him or not."

"But you already—"

Jason's complaint broke off when the third man boxed the back of his head. "Shut the fuck up, or we're gonna use you to show Courtney how hard we can hit."

I shouldn't have been surprised by his use of my name since Jason knew me, but it threw me off even more.

"Repeatedly," the biggest one growled before turning his attention back to me. "You get that we're serious about finding Sabrina?"

My mind was reeling, but I nodded and gulped down the giant lump in my throat. "Yes."

"Good," he grunted as the other two dragged Jason toward the door. "The bitch isn't answering any of his calls, but you better hope like hell she'll answer for you. We'll be back in forty-eight hours, and I expect you to have some answers by then."

Two days was nothing, especially when I already knew that Sabrina wasn't taking my calls either. I had no hope of finding her in such a short time, which only gave me one option to get out of this mess.

Glancing over his shoulder as he neared the door, he warned, "And don't try anything stupid, like going to the cops. We got eyes and ears everywhere, so we'd know that you tried to fuck us over like your roommate. Then our next visit would be a hell of a lot less friendly."

The plan that had been forming in my brain flew out the window with his threat. Calling the police and getting the wrong person wasn't worth the risk.

When the door finally shut behind them, I slumped against the hard surface, tears filling my eyes. I could've used a stiff drink after that scary encounter, but I was only twenty, so I couldn't go out and buy one. And we didn't have anything in the apartment because Sabrina drank her alcohol as quickly as she bought it.

If I made it out of this disaster, I needed to be much more careful when it came to picking my next roommate. Or maybe I would look for a weekend job so I could afford the apartment on my own. Anything would be better than going through something like this again. Assuming I survived the mess Sabrina had left behind.

2
COURTNEY

I was exhausted the following morning when I went to work. After spending most of the night searching every inch of Sabrina's room and our shared space, I only managed to get about three hours of sleep. Getting up and ready for a day at the bank was rough, but I didn't call out sick because I needed to be there to put my new plan into motion.

By the end of my shift, I was a bundle of nerves. The opportunity to look up the information that I needed hadn't come all day long. But with my coworkers focused on reconciling their drawers, I was finally able to run a quick search on the account I was looking for—Hounds of Hellfire MC.

When I crawled into bed to try to get a little sleep at two thirty in the morning, I thought I was doomed because I hadn't found a single clue as to where Sabrina might've gone. The only things she had left behind in her room were uniforms from all the jobs where she'd been fired or quit. I even dug through the pockets, desperate to find the smallest hint of her whereabouts. But there was nothing.

It wasn't until I was half-asleep that it hit me...I'd heard her whispering on her phone a couple of days before she left. Something about the Hounds, which I had thought was an odd term for her to use since she wasn't a fan of dogs. Or cats. Or any kind of pet, really.

It had been the middle of the night, and I was half-asleep while getting up to use the bathroom, so I had just shrugged it off as misunderstanding what she had said. But thinking back on that night, she'd been acting weirder than usual. So I pulled out my laptop and did a little internet sleuthing.

I was surprised to find there was a motorcycle club a few towns over called the Hounds of Hellfire, and I couldn't help but wonder if they were somehow involved in her disappearance. After more digging online, I found no bad stuff about the club. No news reports about trouble they caused or members getting arrested, like what you'd see with motorcycle clubs on television shows. They owned a lot of stuff in Riverstone, including some business names that I recognized from work.

Bluesky was a regional bank, and most locals kept accounts with us. That was also apparently true of the Hounds of Hellfire MC.

Without any other leads, I figured a quick check of the bank's system couldn't hurt as long as I didn't get caught. I hoped I'd find an address listed on an account that wasn't public. Maybe a place where they'd hide a person...or at least some paperwork to help me find Sabrina.

It was a long shot, but desperate times called for desperate measures. And I was stunned to discover that my bet paid off.

There was an account with an address on one of the old county roads owned by the same LLC listed on the bar I'd read about last night, The Open Road. I'd never been out that way, but if the area was anything like the county roads surrounding my town, it would be the perfect place to hide stuff from prying eyes.

I was just about to jot down the address when the teller directly to my left said, "Hey, Courtney."

My head jerked up, and I glanced over at Susie. "Yes?"

"Can you take my shift next Saturday?"

I barely stopped my shoulders from slumping in relief since I had thought she was going to ask me what I was doing. Forcing an apologetic smile, I shook my head. "Sorry, but I already have plans that day."

I didn't really, but it seemed like a better answer than I wasn't sure if I'd even be around to work after tomorrow. If I didn't figure out where Sabrina was, I might be in the hospital. Or worse.

"Darn," she sighed.

"Maybe Paul can cover for you," I suggested, jerking my head toward the teller on the other side of her.

When she turned to ask him, I quickly wrote down the address and clocked out. My guilty conscience got the better of me, and I felt like everyone was staring at me as I said my goodbyes.

On my drive home, I was careful to drive exactly the speed limit. I didn't even have anything incriminating on me, but with how jittery I was feeling, I didn't want to get pulled over.

Parking in my assigned spot, I scanned the lot for any sign of the guys who'd forced their way into my apartment yesterday. When I didn't see anyone, I headed into the building.

I didn't feel any safer inside my apartment, so I

let out a soft shriek when my cell rang. Glancing at the screen, I saw my brother's name. I always answered when he called but was sorely tempted to send him to voicemail. Arlen took his big brother duties seriously, and I knew I couldn't avoid him for long. His Navy SEAL team was due to deploy overseas soon, so he'd want an update on how things were going for me before he left.

I briefly considered telling him about what was going on, but I didn't want to stress him out right before he went into a potentially dangerous situation. Not until after I checked out that address first, at least. If I didn't turn up anything on Sabrina, then I'd think about calling Arlen to ask for help before my forty-eight hours were up.

"Hey, big bro. How're you doing?" I asked, infusing my voice with an enthusiasm I didn't feel.

I should've known it wouldn't work because Arlen was too observant for my own good. "What's wrong?"

"Just a long day at work. Sometimes people can be such jerks."

Both statements were true, they just weren't the whole story.

"You need me to come teach 'em a lesson the next time I'm on leave?"

I wasn't surprised by his offer since he'd always been protective of me, and it had only amped up when our parents passed away in a car crash shortly after I graduated from high school. I gave him the same answer I'd done each time he'd said something similar. "I'll let you know if it comes down to needing that."

"You better."

"Enough about me. Anything new going on with you that you can actually tell me about? Like maybe you met my future sister-in-law?" I asked, knowing that questions about his love life—or lack thereof—would sidetrack him from grilling me about what was going on with me.

"Like I have time to worry about dating," he growled.

"All I'm hearing are excuses," I chided. "Especially when so many of the guys on your team are happily married."

With how demanding their job was, the divorce rates for Navy SEALs tended to be really high. But a lot of the men my brother worked with had defied the odds, which gave me hope for whenever he found the special woman who made him fall head over heels in love for the first time. Not that I blamed him for holding out for the right one. Our parents had set a high bar for relationships since they hadn't hidden from us how deeply in love they'd been with each other.

"Yeah, yeah," he grumbled, changing the topic to mundane stuff.

We chatted for about five more minutes before he had to go. "Love you, sis."

"Love you, too," I choked out, barely resisting the urge to blurt out everything that was going on.

Instead, I hung up and waited until after sunset to drive to the warehouse located on the south side of Riverstone. I'd never broken into anywhere before, but I assumed that doing it in broad daylight upped the odds of getting caught.

When it was finally dark out, I dressed in all black and headed out to my car. Then I carefully drove to the address I'd pulled off the bank's computer and hoped like heck that I wasn't going to their compound because then I'd have zero chance of sneaking in. Or at least I assumed I would, based on the little I knew about motorcycle clubs. All of which I'd learned from television shows or the online research I'd done over the past few hours.

I drove past the address, peering out my passenger side window and heaving a deep sigh of relief when I didn't spot a single car or person anywhere. There was a guard shack, but no lights were on inside.

The gate was closed, so I took advantage of the lack of traffic to slowly circle the property until I found a spot where I could pull my car next to the fence. I hopped out and climbed onto the hood, then crawled up to the roof, which gave me just enough of a boost to make it over the top rail. After landing on the other side, I ran as fast as I could toward the large building, glad for just enough moonlight to see where I was going.

When I reached the back door, I leaned against the hard surface, gasping for breath. I tried the handle and found it locked. I jiggled it a few times with a groan before pounding my head against the door. Patting my pocket, I was grateful that my brother had drilled into my head to always carry a multi-tool pocket knife.

Between that, my flashlight, and a handy video online that I streamed on my phone, I was able to pick the lock using the scissors. All I had to do was flip the handle down so it lined up with one of the blades. Then I inserted it into the keyhole, jiggling up and down while pressing toward the opening. Eventually, I was able to turn the tool to the right, unlocking the door.

"Holy crap, I can't believe that worked," I breathed as I yanked the scissors out of the lock, closing it before tucking it back in my pocket, along with my phone.

Quickly opening the door, I crept inside and slammed it shut behind me. The huge place was eerily silent, but I shook off my unease and took several steps forward. There were lots of tall metal shelves with bins and boxes, but nothing that looked out of the ordinary. As I swept the beam of light in a circle, I spotted an office about a hundred feet to my right.

I raced in that direction, only stopping as I passed a door that had a maintenance sign on it. Some instinct told me to peek inside, and Arlen had taught me to always listen to my gut. Looking inside, I found a bunch of cleaning supplies. But more importantly, there was an electrical panel.

I wasn't sure what kind of alarm system the Hounds of Hellfire had on this warehouse, but turning off the power sounded like a good idea.

Once that was done, I went to the office, relieved to find this door unlocked. Letting myself inside, I gaped at the long row of filing cabinets lining one of the walls.

"Darn it," I groaned.

This would take longer than I thought, but leaving now wasn't an option. Propping my flashlight in my armpit, I got to work on going through the files and searching for Sabrina's name on any of the paperwork. I was about halfway through them when my flashlight suddenly turned off.

I shook it a few times, but nothing happened. "You have to be kidding me."

I didn't think to bring extra batteries, so I tucked the useless thing into my back pocket and stalked toward the nearest window. Yanking open the blinds, I glanced back at the filing cabinet to see if there was enough moonlight for me to see what I was doing. Unfortunately, there wasn't.

It was also too dark for me to make it back to the door I used to get into the warehouse, so I opened the window since it was the closest way out of the building. Then I remembered having the lighter Arlen told me to always carry. My brother never would've guessed his instructions would come in handy while I was breaking and entering, and I hoped to never need to tell him.

Determined to find a way out of this predicament, I lit the flame and continued searching. The improvisation slowed my pace, but it worked...until I moved the lighter too close to the stack of papers I was reading and one of them caught on fire. Before I could put it out, the flame quickly jumped to the nearest row of folders.

"Crap, crap, crap," I chanted, frantically searching the office for a fire extinguisher.

I had passed a couple as I crept through the warehouse in search of the office, but I hadn't expected to need them, so I hadn't paid much attention to their location.

Instead of finding something to help get me out of a bad situation, I'd only made matters worse, literally setting my life on fire.

3

BLAZE

"Blaze."

I halted in my tracks and looked back over my shoulder to see King, the president of my motorcycle club, The Hounds of Hellfire, walking toward me.

"You going by the warehouse on the south side today?" he asked, a scowl on his face. Pretty much his natural expression unless he was looking at his old lady, Stella. They were a little nauseating with their happiness and palpable sexual tension. But as much as I enjoyed giving them shit about it, I couldn't help being just a little jealous.

"Yeah. Smoke detectors need the batteries changed, and I want to check on the new dry chemical fire suppression system I just installed."

I'd inspected it a couple of days ago, so it was probably overkill, but I could be a bit fanatical when it came to fire safety. This particular warehouse was mostly storage for documents, so I'd replaced our old wet pipe system to avoid water damage to the structure and hopefully, all the paperwork.

"Ace dropped these by my office earlier," he told me, holding out a manila folder. "Backup employee tax documents for The Open Road. Need them filed while you're there."

Ace was our treasurer and financial guru. Lately, he'd been holed up in his office working on the taxes for our legal businesses, including the bar we owned in our little town of Riverstone, Georgia.

I took the file and waved it. "No problem."

Before I could turn away, he spoke again. "By the way, the Georgia DNR called."

I sighed. "Again?"

This was the third time they'd called me in as many months. They wanted help with another controlled burn. It was something I assisted with from time to time. Usually when they were in areas that had not been burned in a long time because special attention was required when reintroducing fire. Which was why they called me.

After high school, I went into the military and eventually earned a PhD in combustion science. I became a pyrologist and worked as an arson investigator, but I was also a demolitions expert. It was how I got the road name "Blaze" when I patched with the Hounds. That and the many fires I'd set as a delinquent kid.

Those talents came in very handy with my other activities for the Hounds. But those tasks were being interrupted by calls from the Department of Natural Resources. For some reason, they'd chosen to tackle some of the most neglected areas this season.

I hated to turn them down, but the MC came first, and I had a fucking job to do.

"I'll call Jack Glazner before I leave," I told King. "They want my help, they'll have to wait. This run is time-sensitive."

King shook his head. "Don't worry about it. I'll handle the DNR. Just get on the road. Echo has the paperwork, and Kevlar is carrying the necessary supplies. Keep the footprint small, don't want to draw too much attention." A rare smile curved the prez's lips. "Maybe check around the house for any fireworks before you light the flame."

"One damn time that happened," I growled and pivoted around, stalking toward the lounge, where there was an exit into the garage. The client should have warned me that there was a stash of aerial fireworks in the fucking kitchen pantry.

When the flames reached the skyrockets, we'd been long gone. But my brothers just couldn't let my oversight the fuck go after hearing about how some of them made it into the sky where they exploded, raining colorful sparks over the house.

Our sergeant at arms, Kevlar, and Road Captain, Echo, were waiting for me in the garage. I lifted my chin in greeting, then mounted my hog, and we took off.

The place we were visiting was about an hour out of town. It was an office building set in a business complex. Luckily, most of the other companies who'd occupied the surrounding buildings had moved on a couple of years ago.

A man waited for us at the rear entrance when we arrived. We parked our bikes, and after hopping off, I grabbed the shit I needed from a saddlebag and walked straight for the door, letting Echo handle the client.

The guy was an accountant and had stumbled across some questions with the books. When he dug deeper, he discovered money laundering happening within the company. He brought it to the attention of the wrong people, and now he had a price on his head.

The man was a cocky son of a bitch, so I'd been a little surprised that he was the honest one among the bunch. From the wiretap we'd put on the CEO's phone, it turned out our client had even been offered a bribe—a very generous one—and he'd turned it down. But Echo had a fuck of a lot more patience than I did, which was why he was the one handling the whistleblower.

He'd come to the Hounds of Hellfire because we were known for our ability and willingness to help people disappear...for the right price. Not that we turned away everyone who couldn't pay, but these gigs were a huge part of our livelihood.

We had several legitimate businesses, but most of the time, we adhered to our own laws. Our brand of justice included crossing lines drawn by a flawed legal system. Sometimes even the local police looked the other way when we could accomplish something they didn't have the authority or connections to handle.

Donations from the MC to the police fund hadn't hurt that cause either. We weren't ones to buy politicians, but having friends in high places made many of our jobs easier.

The building had no surveillance, and Wizard—our tech genius—had diverted any satellite footage. So I was free to go to work without worrying about staying invisible. After putting everything in place, and doing a thorough search of the building, I ambled outside and waited for my brothers near our bikes.

We'd already handled the "death" of the client, providing a body from one of the coroners we worked with. It had similar characteristics and the same build as our guy. We'd also laid the groundwork for it to appear as if he was being pursued by multiple organizations, then made the body appear unrecognizable from torture. Wizard had done his magic, changing the DNA, dental, and medical records to match our client. Now, I was getting rid of the evidence he'd discovered.

The guy had been afraid of having only digital copies, but our servers were more secure than the CIA's. We even had a SKIFF room for any sensitive information that needed extra protection. Wizard had the digital files, so I'd prepped a small electrical fire that would burn the paperwork before the sprinkler system put it out so the flames wouldn't spread beyond my chosen perimeter.

After so many years as an arson investigator, I

knew how to get away with all kinds of shit. When it came to fire, I was the best.

Kevlar loaded his bike into the back of a nondescript truck and took off with the client. He'd ensure the guy made it to whatever transportation would take him to his new life.

Echo walked around the building for a final perimeter check, then strode over to where I straddled my bike.

"Think he'll follow our instructions?" I asked casually. This client was an asshole and had been very obstinate, trying to tell us how to do our fucking jobs when he didn't know shit about what we did.

Echo shrugged. "Pretty sure King scared the fuck outta him the other day, but who the hell knows? Jackass might have blown the whistle on those fuckers, but if he ends up sinking to the bottom of the Atlantic for running his mouth, it wouldn't surprise me."

"Nah," I disagreed with a shake of my head. "They're more of the bury the body in concrete type."

Echo chuckled and mounted his motorcycle, then we rode back toward the clubhouse. About ten minutes from the compound, I turned onto a different road to the south side of town, where the warehouse was located.

A minute before the building came into view, I received an alert on my watch that a fire detector was going off.

What the fuck?

I briefly wondered if it was a false alarm due to a battery malfunction, then tossed that theory because that wasn't how they worked.

However, false alarms due to other factors had been a problem from time to time, just like any fire system, which was why the warnings came to me before the fire department. We preferred that no one except Hounds, patches, or prospects set foot on our property. If the issue could be handled without the fire department's help, we didn't involve them.

I pulled up to the guard shack, which was empty as I expected. We didn't man it unless there was a meeting or something happening. As I glanced up at the large structure, I let out a string of curses when I saw smoke billowing out of a back window. One that shouldn't have been open.

By the time I rolled through the gate, the smoke coming out of the window had been replaced by flames.

Fuck.

4

BLAZE

My eyes scanned the building as I ran toward the front entrance. The flames were growing, which shouldn't have been happening because the suppression system should have kicked on already. But I hadn't received that alert, meaning there was probably a malfunction.

Shit! Shit! Shit!

Since the fire still seemed to be contained in that section of the building, I tied a bandanna around my face and one around my hand before I unlocked the heavy metal door and yanked it open.

I'd run a system check two days before, so it made no sense that it wasn't working.

As I ran inside, I frowned when the motion lights didn't activate. The door slammed shut, leaving me in mostly darkness, causing me to pause—not that I had time to spare—so my eyes could adjust. I flipped the nearest switch and nothing happened. What the hell was going on? Was the electricity out?

The electrical panel was in a maintenance closet on the left side of the building. The same side as the growing flames, but there was no time to waste, so I took off in that direction.

When I reached the room, I didn't bother turning the knob. I just kicked the door open and rushed over to see that the panel door was open and the main switch had been flipped. *Motherfucker!*

If the power was off, it might have explained the system failure. The fire pump could have failed to engage. Except, by law, fire pumps had to be hooked up to an emergency generator, so it should have been working. Unless there was a hiccup in the fucking generator.

The exit to the loading dock was near the back of the building, so I cursed a blue streak as I raced to the door. I heard the sudden shattering of glass—probably the windows exploding from the heat.

Outside, the generator was hooked up next to the concrete pad, and I hurried over to it. I turned it off and held down the reset button, wincing when I heard another window blow. It took a few seconds, but the error messages on the control panel disappeared. It restarted as soon as I turned it on, thank fuck.

Seconds later, I got the alert that the fire suppression system went online. I exhaled a harsh breath in relief and turned to walk away from the burning building when I heard a crash and a scream.

I whipped back around and ran for the door, wondering who the fuck was inside. It had come from the direction of the flames, and though I probably should have thought twice before running into a fire, I had to find the person trapped inside.

The fire seemed to be contained to two rooms, and the flames had eaten away the wall between them. A tall file cabinet was on the ground, most likely because it had crashed through the weakening wall. Thankfully, the powder sprayed from the localized sprinklers had already lessened the intensity of the flames.

I made a beeline for the room that seemed to have the most damage, assuming that whoever was trapped had been the cause of the fire. Just as I reached the door, a body came flying out, ramming into me and nearly knocking us both to the floor.

Even with the inferno easing, I didn't waste time

scooping the person into my arms and racing to the closest exit.

After bursting out of the back door into the moonlight, I kept running until we were far enough away that any structural damage or falling debris wouldn't reach us.

My adrenaline was high as fuck, my heart thumping, and my rage was burning as hot as the fire we'd just escaped.

I dropped the person onto their feet and grabbed their shoulders, barely seeing them in front of me through my red haze of fury. "The fuck did you do? Were you trying to kill yourself?" I shouted.

"It was an accident, I swear!"

The feminine voice sent a shock wave through my body that had nothing to do with the anger or the residual effects from running in and out of a burning building.

I shook my head, trying to clear away the confusing reaction.

"You broke in to my warehouse and set a fucking fire on accident?" I growled.

She blinked at me, and despite the soot darkening her pale skin, pink bloomed on her cheeks. "Well, um, the fire was an accident."

Her hazel orbs were filled with apprehension,

but I still had to fight not to get lost in the beautiful mixture of green and blue. They were rimmed with black lashes that matched her midnight-black hair. It was pulled back in a ponytail, but it was long and thick. The moonlight made it look like silk, making my hands itch to yank it down and shove my fingers into the strands.

What the fuck was wrong with me?

I silently scolded myself to stop ogling my little arsonist and get my head back in the game.

"Then what were you doing?"

She glanced away and shuffled her feet, telling me that whatever answer she gave me would most likely be a lie.

"You got any idea who you were robbing, baby?" I seethed. For some reason, the idea of her getting tangled up with the wrong MC pissed me off as much as the fire she set.

The woman gasped and poked a soot-covered finger in my chest. "I'm not a thief!"

I raised an eyebrow and jabbed my thumb toward the warehouse, which was damaged, but thankfully, no longer on fire. "Breaking and entering says otherwise."

"Okay, so that doesn't exactly look good for me,"

she mumbled. "And my name is Courtney, not baby."

As pissed as I was, I held back a smile at her snippy tone, which was in direct contrast to her deep blush. But then the sight of the soot and grime on her cheeks made me think of what could have happened to her if I hadn't come to the warehouse tonight.

Just like that, I was back to being enraged.

"Answer the question, baby," I snarled.

She scowled and crossed her arms over her chest, bringing my attention to her tits. They weren't big, but they fit with her slender curves and would fill my hands perfectly.

For fuck's sake! My irritation level was growing the more I was distracted by Courtney's body. She had nearly burned down our building and herself in the process. That needed to be my fucking focus.

When she remained stubbornly silent, my patience expired.

"Let's go," I grunted, clasping her arm so I could lead her around the building to my bike.

But she dug in her heels and yelled, "You can't take me to the police!"

I rolled my eyes and spun around to face her. "Not going to the cops, baby. You've got your pretty little ass mixed up with much worse."

Her expression was wary when she insisted, "I'm not afraid of you."

Moving close, I stopped when we were almost nose to nose. "You fucking should be." Not me or a single member of my MC would ever hurt her, but I was not above using intimidation tactics to get what I wanted.

"You caused a fucking fire that could've gotten your ass killed and did some serious damage to a Hounds of Hellfire building."

"I told you," she cried, throwing her hands in the air. "I didn't mean to cause a fire! I just needed—" She stopped and pressed her lips together.

"Needed what?"

Her mutinous expression said she wasn't gonna explain.

If I was going to get some fucking answers from Courtney, I needed to get us both back to the compound. Just standing out here wasn't gonna motivate her to be honest. Besides, seeing all the destruction that would have to be fixed was just pissing me off even more.

"Let's go," I grunted again. When she dug her feet in, I released her arm and grabbed her waist, tossing her over my shoulder.

"Hey!" she squealed. "Put me down!"

"No."

"You can't just kidnap me!"

"You gonna tell me what the fuck you were doing here?"

Silence.

"Then I sure as hell can."

She shouted and flailed as I stalked around the building until I smacked her ass.

Courtney gasped, but I didn't give her a chance to say anything. I flipped her off my shoulder and plunked her down on the seat of my hog. Then I climbed on behind her. It was safer for her to sit behind me, but I didn't want her hopping off anytime we hit a stoplight.

I reached down and pulled a helmet from one of my saddlebags and put it on her. Then I leaned around to fasten it.

Even with the smell of smoke permeating our skin and clothes, I could discern a hint of something sweet.

Once we were both settled, she started to speak again, but the roar of the engine drowned her out.

It wasn't a long ride to the compound, but it was enough for me to recognize that Courtney's body fit perfectly into the groove of mine, like she was made just for me.

And it was more than enough time for me to know that she was mine.

I lifted my chin at Ink, a recent patch who was operating the guard shack. He'd seen me coming and had the gate open.

His eyes drifted to my passenger, and his brow rose. I ignored him and rode through, only stopping once I'd pulled my bike into the garage.

"Where are we?" She moved as if to get off, but I grabbed her waist and held her still.

I needed a fucking minute after having her perfect ass snuggled up against me.

"We'll talk inside," I rasped.

"But—"

Growling in frustration, I hopped off the bike and scooped her into my arms. She wiggled and twisted, muttering under her breath.

"Stop squirming and be quiet," I snapped, squeezing her closer to my body.

Courtney stilled and huffed, "Will you—"

"Not. Another. Word."

I stormed into the clubhouse and through the lounge where King, his old lady—Stella—and a few of my brothers were hanging out.

"What the fuck?" King grunted.

"Gonna need to schedule a construction crew to

head out to the warehouse on the south side of town," I muttered without missing a step as I headed toward the stairs to the second floor where my living quarters were located. "The sprinkler system I had us put in did its job"—*once it was turned on*, I thought darkly—"but the place is gonna need a fuck of a lot of work."

Courtney writhed in my hold again, causing me to hold her even tighter so she could barely move. "I'm—"

"I already told you, not another word," I growled before looking at King. "Tell Ace that I'm good for the cost," I grunted, referring to our treasurer. "Whatever it is. Don't want this run through insurance." If we reported this shit, they would involve the police. Courtney was mine, so I'd handle the situation and make sure she didn't end up in jail.

"Will do, man," King called out as I stomped up the steps.

At the top of the stairs, I turned right and stalked down to the end.

King lived in a house the previous president had built onto the back of the clubhouse. But my quarters were closer to the rooms occupied by the other patches who lived on-site.

However, mine were different from most of the others.

A lot of them were similar to a dorm room, even using shared bathrooms. Some had a private bath and others a small kitchenette.

As the VP, my "room" was a one-bedroom apartment.

I unlocked the door and went inside, slamming it behind me. After securing the lock, I marched to the bedroom and unceremoniously dumped Courtney onto my king-sized bed. Now, it was time to get some answers.

5

COURTNEY

I had hopped straight from the frying pan into the hellfire. Instead of needing to worry about those guys who had visited my apartment with Jason yesterday, I now had to be concerned about the fact that I'd been caught by a member of the Hounds of Hellfire while breaking in—and setting fire to—their warehouse. And not just anyone, but their vice president, based on the patch on the front of his leather vest.

The name above it was particularly appropriate, considering he had just saved me from a burning building. And his gray eyes burned as he stared down at me, his hands planted on his narrow hips. The position was intimidating, and he wasn't the kind of guy who needed any advantages in that arena. Or any other one from what I could see.

Between the eight extra inches he had on me, the muscles, the hint of black ink I caught on his forearm, and his super-short brown hair...he was tall, dark, and dangerous personified. And the first man who'd ever brought my libido roaring to life.

Even right now, when my life might very well hang in the balance from two different threats—him being one of them—I found it difficult to resist Blaze's lure. He'd spanked me, tossed me onto his motorcycle, and forced me to come to his compound. And yelled at me in front of his friends before carting me to his room. But none of that made him less sexy. Only more so, if anything.

"You gonna tell me what the fuck you were doing at our warehouse?" he growled.

The dampening of my panties was a completely inappropriate reaction to his question. It left me feeling irritated and confused, and for some reason, I decided to throw him some sass in an effort to cover it up. Sitting up, I crossed my arms over my chest. "You told me not to say another word, remember?"

Shaking his head with a laugh, he arched a brow. "Your feistiness is cute, baby. And sexy as hell, but you know damn well I didn't mean for you to give me the silent treatment once I finally got you somewhere we could talk without anyone hearing what you have to say for yourself. Can't protect you until I know why the fuck you were at our warehouse or how you accidentally started the fire. So talk."

Even with those last two gruff words, I was melting inside over the fact that he wanted to protect me. Especially with how we met since I couldn't have left a good impression. Or even a halfway decent one.

I scooted to the end of the mattress and let my legs dangle off the edge. "I don't even know where to begin."

"How did the fire start?" he asked, pacing back and forth in front of his bed.

I guessed that spot was as good as any, so I yanked my flashlight out of my pocket and shook it. "My batteries died, and I needed to be able to see what I was doing. Since I cut the power just in case you had a security system, I couldn't turn on the lights. So I used a lighter, and the next thing I knew, the papers I was holding caught on fire. Everything quickly spiraled out of control from there."

"Fire has a way of doing that," he muttered. "Why were you looking in our files in the first place?"

It was wild that the part about how I'd set fire to his warehouse was the easiest part of my explanation. "Okay, so...this is going to sound like I'm making up a story to get out of trouble, but I swear I'm telling the truth."

"It's that bad?" he asked, dropping onto the mattress beside me.

"Bad doesn't even begin to describe it," I grumbled before going into everything that happened yesterday when Jason and those three guys forced their way into my apartment.

"How long ago did your roommate disappear?"

I gave him the timeline of the last time I saw Sabrina and also explained how I remembered her mentioning the Hounds on the phone, searched the bank's system, and found the warehouse's address. "And that's why I broke in to search the files I found. It was a stretch, but I only have one more day left before they come looking for me, so I was desperate to find anything to help me figure out where Sabrina went. Or even just what she stole from her boyfriend before she disappeared."

"How did you get into the warehouse?" His eyes narrowed. "The security needs to be updated on that building, but I know for a fact the doors were all locked and there aren't any gaps in the fence."

I pulled my multi-tool knife out of my pocket and showed him the scissors with a bashful smile. "It turns out that these are perfectly sized and shaped for lock picking."

"That was resourceful of you," he drawled. I could've sworn that I spied a glint of approval in his gray eyes, but I assumed I'd imagined it.

"Maybe." I shrugged with a sigh. "But I'm still no match for those guys who beat up Jason."

His expression didn't give anything away as he asked, "What did they look like?"

"Big and scary." I squeezed my eyes shut as I tried to remember as many details as possible. "All three of them had dark hair. The biggest one had a full beard. The guy who grabbed me—"

"Grabbed you?" Blaze echoed.

"Um, yeah. He tugged me into my apartment."

"Where?" he growled.

My head tilted to the side. "Where what?"

"Where did he grab you?"

I lifted my elbow to look at my bicep. "My arm."

"Let me see." He gently rolled up my sleeve to check for a bruise, brushing his thumb against my bare skin. "It's good he didn't leave a mark. I might not kill him. But he still had no right to touch you. Which one did it?"

I gave him the rest of the details I remembered, and then he asked for Jason's last name and everything I knew about my roommate.

"Fucking hell." He scraped his palm over his cheek. "You weren't kidding when you said that it was bad."

"I really wasn't," I murmured with a shrug. "And that was before I set fire to your warehouse, for which I owe you a huge apology. I'm so sorry. I hope it looks worse than it is."

"I hate to break it to you, baby, but the damage will be more than you expect."

"Do you really think so?" I asked, my stomach in knots.

"Yeah," he confirmed with a nod. "And I know what I'm talking about because fire is my business."

I cocked my head to the side and stared at him, confused. "Your business?"

He nodded. "I'm a pyrologist. I work with all types of burns—controlled forest fires, explosives and demolition, and I even worked as an arson investigator."

I dropped my head into my hands with a groan. "Oh my gosh. Of course I got caught by a freaking arson investigator when I accidentally started a fire while breaking and entering. I've never committed a crime before, not even jaywalking. And now I'm a...a felon."

"They say go big or go home," he chuckled. "And you sure as fuck did that."

Wincing at the thought of how long it would take me to do it, I offered, "I can pay for the damage. Somehow."

"Don't worry, I got it covered."

"That's nice of you, but—"

"Wasn't being nice, baby," he interrupted. Then he shook his head. "Don't think anyone would use that word to describe me."

My brows drew together. "I don't get it. You just said there's probably a lot more damage than I expect, and I assumed there was a ton. Why are you so insistent that you'll take care of it for me?"

"Because I take care of what's mine."

My breath caught in my throat at his answer, butterflies swirling in my belly. I didn't know how to respond, but that didn't matter because he didn't give me the chance.

Standing, he wrapped his hand around my wrist and tugged me to my feet. "Not good for you to sit around with all of that soot on you. It's best to wash it off as soon as possible to limit absorption into your skin. Go take a shower."

I glanced down at my hands, which were streaked with black gunk that matched my outfit. "At least I was wearing long sleeves." Lifting a lock of my hair, I sniffed it with a grimace. "But that smoke smell is probably going to linger forever."

"Use conditioner first. It works surprisingly well at removing soot." He nudged me toward a closed door to our left.

"Will do." I swept my hand down the length of my body. "But there's one problem. I have nothing to wear, and my clothes are pretty much ruined."

His eyes darkened to the color of slate as his gaze raked over me. "I'll get you something to put on."

"Thanks, I really appreciate it, Blaze."

"Pax."

I had no idea what that meant. "Pardon?"

"You call me Pax, not Blaze."

"Oh, okay." A thought suddenly struck me, and I blushed. "And I'm Courtney Cartwright. No nickname or anything, just Courtney."

He smirked. "Like I said...so fucking cute."

The color in my cheeks deepened as I padded over to the bathroom. After I shut the door behind me, I leaned back against the hard surface. "Whoa."

6

BLAZE

My hands clenched and unclenched as I stared at the closed bathroom door.

The squeak of the faucet as it was turned on, the hiss from the spray of water, the screech of the shower curtain sliding along the bar...every sound made my heart pound harder.

Wet. Naked. Mine.

Fuck!

I had to get the hell outta the room before I barged into the shower and took her up against the wall.

After taking several deep breaths and thinking about anything that would make my dick a little less painful, I stalked over to my dresser and pulled open the top drawer. My clothes would be huge on her, but they would have to do. I briefly considered asking to borrow an outfit from Stella, but the idea of Courtney being surrounded by me was too appealing.

I fished out a pair of boxers, found a T-shirt that was snug on me, and tossed them onto the bed. Then I forced my feet to move toward the door where I paused to throw one last look at the bathroom before stalking out.

Knowing I needed to update my brothers, I sent a text to Wizard and a couple of our enforcers as I quickly made my way back downstairs. When I saw King still in the lounge, I jerked my chin in the direction of our offices and kept walking without waiting to see if he followed.

Ace was at his desk as I passed by and rapped my knuckles on his doorjamb. "Prez's. Now," I called. "Bring Ash."

When I got there, I stopped beside King's desk and faced the door, standing with my feet braced apart and my arms crossed over my chest.

King entered and rounded his desk to take a seat. He was followed into the room by Echo and Ace, who both settled themselves on the couch in the small lounge area on the side of the room, opposite the conference table.

"So..." Echo drawled with a smirk. "Was I right?"

"About what?" I grunted.

"You falling for a wannabe arsonist?" He laughed, and I scowled.

"That's funny because...?"

Echo looked over at King, his smirk back in place. "Gonna have to tell Stella I was right," he practically crowed. Then his gaze returned to me, and he tilted his head, studying me. "Gotta say, Blaze claiming a firebug is a little cliché."

"Shut your mouth, E," King growled. "Unless you wanna lose that pretty-boy face of yours."

Echo's eyes darted from our prez to me, and when he clocked my dark scowl, he pressed his lips together as if suppressing a laugh. One more word and I was gonna do exactly what King had suggested.

When he didn't say anything else, I focused my attention on the door. I didn't want to have to share all this shit more than once, so we all waited in awkward silence until Wizard strolled into the office with Ash—our secretary, who was a lawyer and handled all the MC's legal shit—and a couple of our enforcers, Rebel and Tomcat.

"I take it you're going to explain about the warehouse and the woman you brought here?" King asked.

Before I could answer, Echo snorted, and I glared at him. "More like kidnapped."

King shot him a look, and he shut up, but as he leaned back into the cushions, a grin spread across his face.

"What's going on?" King asked me.

After I explained the situation, Rebel whistled softly. "Damn. That's seriously fucked up."

"No shit," I grunted. Shifting my gaze to Wizard, I asked, "Was the roommate a client?"

Wizard nodded and opened his laptop, setting it on the conference room table where he'd sat when he showed up. "Yeah. Pulled her file from the skiff room server."

I scowled and clenched my hands into fists. "Can't expect everyone who comes to us to be completely clean, I get that. But how the fuck did this bitch slip through our deep dive into her background?"

He tapped a few keys, and his eyes scanned the screen. "Wasn't thrilled with her history or the people she associated with, but she was mostly just a random chick with nothing that indicated she might be running from a drug ring. Claimed to be tryin' to get away from the ex, and since he has a long list of assault charges, her story was plausible."

"Why didn't we find out where she got the money to pay us?" I muttered.

Ace piped up. "That was my call. I did ask Wizard about Jason since he was obviously in the ranks of this drug ring. When he told me the guy was low on the ladder, I figured the likelihood of her getting anywhere near product or money was extremely low. Still not sure how she could have gotten her hands on either. So I sent it to King for the green light."

"Do we know where she is?" I asked, frustrated with Ace's answer even though it made sense.

Wizard tapped some keys on his computer and shook his head. "We used Ink's connection with the DeLucas to find her a place. I'll have to get the information from them."

One of our recent patches was related to a New York crime family run by Nic DeLuca. They had a branch of The Family in the south, mostly in Georgia, not far from Riverstone. The connection had turned into a great working relationship since both of our organizations had skills the other lacked but needed.

"She opened her legs for far too many lowlife motherfuckers. Not just gangs or drug pushers, that includes dirty MCs. There were too many risks that she would be recognized in our circles. So The Family erased her through their channels."

"Get Ink on it," I ordered, then looked at Ace. "She pay cash?"

"Yeah, but the bills were new and sequential. Wizard and I can follow the money."

"Do it."

They both stood and were already throwing theories at each other by the time they walked out the door.

Once they were gone, Ash tapped his fingers on the table impatiently. "Tell me about the warehouse. How much shit was destroyed?"

I winced. "Pretty much everything in the filing rooms on one side of the building."

"Fuck," he muttered.

"We have digital duplicates of everything," King reminded him.

"I know. But being able to hand over paper copies has saved our asses when someone like the IRS has come sniffing around. Kept them off our servers, and the idiots never suspect that the 'originals' could have been tampered with."

King nodded. "Get some prospects to reprint and organize the files."

"Will do," Ash agreed. "And we're still keeping the fire off the record?"

I grunted in affirmation. "Can't trust the cops we don't know. Any of them could have their balls in a vise by that organization."

"I'll talk to the sheriff," Tomcat offered. He was a former Navy pilot and had been in the academy with the county sheriff's brother. The officer, Bruce, was a pretty straight arrow, but he respected the fuck out of Tomcat, and they were good friends. So when Tomcat patched, Bruce did his due diligence and checked us out. Since it was handy to have law enforcement on your side—sort of—we gave him a little more access than we would give most outsiders.

He fed us information we needed from time to time, and if the circumstances were right, he'd been known to look the other way when we needed him to.

"Thanks."

Tomcat gave me a chin lift.

"Blaze."

I looked at King, who was studying his computer screen. "How'd she get in?"

One side of my mouth quirked up. "She picked the lock."

King glanced up at me with a raised brow. "Picked the lock?"

I nodded, feeling a spark of pride even though I should've been pissed that someone had broken into our facility. Courtney was a fascinating tangle of personality types. I had a feeling that even in a whole lifetime with her, I'd never unravel them all.

"Told you we needed more security than that fucking fence and some locks," Rebel groused. He was in charge of security for the Hounds—a job he was perfect for after being a SEAL specializing in security.

"I signed the check, Rebel," King murmured as he leaned back in his chair. "The new system is scheduled to be installed next week."

Rebel snorted. "Little late."

"So the bill for the warehouse repairs goes to you?"

My eyes narrowed as my head turned in Ace's direction. His voice was amused, and when I met his eyes, they were full of laughter.

"Yeah," I muttered, intending to leave it at that.

"Trying to save us on an insurance premium hike?"

"No," I snapped.

"Oh?" His expression and tone were overly innocent.

King sighed. "Cruisin' for a bruisin', jackass."

"You know why, fucker."

"Still gonna make you say it."

I dropped my hands to my sides, both curled into fists, and took a step toward Ace.

"For fuck's sake, Ace," King muttered. "Not gonna stop him if he decides to kick your ass."

"Why are you paying for the damage?" Rebel asked in his usual low, rough tone that matched his perpetual scowl. He seemed genuinely curious, and I had to remind myself that the prez was the only one in the room who understood what I was experiencing.

"Taking care of what's mine," I growled before stomping away.

7

COURTNEY

"Pax?" I called after stepping out of the shower and wrapping the towel around my body.

When he didn't answer, I tucked the corner between my breasts and slowly opened the door a few inches. I didn't see him in the room, so I cautiously stepped inside and walked over to the bed. A T-shirt and pair of boxers were waiting for me on the mattress.

After putting them on, I shook my head with a soft laugh. The boxers were so wide on my hips that I had to roll them up twice, and the shirt came all the way down to my mid-thigh.

Only a moment later, the door opened, and Pax walked into the room. My cheeks heated, thinking about how he would have found me if he'd only been a few minutes faster.

"Hey," I whispered.

His eyes turned molten as his gaze swept down my body. "That shirt has never looked so good."

I ducked my head and tucked a lock of hair behind my ear. "Thanks for leaving it out for me."

"Willing to bet you'd be more comfortable if you had pants and other girly shit, so I'll ask Stella to get you some stuff."

"Who's Stella?" I asked, a little disgruntled over how easily he mentioned her.

"She's King's old lady," he explained. "He's our prez and one of my best friends. Known him since we were punk kids, doing stupid shit together because we both had a shitty home life."

His gaze zeroed in on where my fingers were toying with the bottom of the shirt that he'd loaned me, and I dropped the soft material. "I'm sorry to hear that."

"It is what it is." He shrugged. "If I hadn't been looking for something I couldn't find at home, I never would've met King. Or Pierce."

I perched on the edge of the bed, tugging the shirt so that the bottom covered my knees. "Who's Pierce?"

"He was the prez of the Hounds before King." He shook his head with a deep chuckle. "And the guy who pulled our heads outta our asses when we were younger. Taught us a fuckuva lot along the way, too."

"He sounds like he was quite a man."

"Still is." At my look of surprise, he added, "Pierce was a hell of a president, but he's an even better grandpa. And great-grandpa now. Six years ago, he decided to hand the reins over to King so he could spend more time with all of 'em without needing to worry about club business."

My lips curved into a soft smile as I pictured a gray-haired mountain of a biker surrounded by a passel of little kids. "Sounds like a smart plan to me."

"He was always good with those."

"What's ours?" I asked.

He gestured toward the black streaks on his face. "Got to get cleaned up. Then I don't know about you, but I'm wiped. So we sleep on the situation for tonight and figure out our next step in the morning."

I had zero interest in going back home, but I was willing to go along with whatever Pax wanted. The man had saved me from a burning building, didn't turn me over to the police when it was exactly what I deserved, and refused to hear a word about me paying for any of the damage. "Do you have another vehicle other than your bike?"

His brows drew together. "I do, but what does that have to do with anything?"

"I just figured that I can't ride on the back of your bike dressed like this," I explained, pointing at my bare legs.

"We're not going anywhere," he replied with a shake of his head as he kicked off his boots. "It isn't safe for you to go back to your apartment, so you're gonna stay here."

"By here, do you mean in this room? With you?" I tugged my bottom lip between my teeth, both nervous and excited at the prospect of sharing a bed with him tonight.

"That's exactly what I mean," he confirmed, reaching out to tug my lip free. "Let go. If anyone is going to bruise your perfect mouth, it's gonna be me."

"Holy crap," I breathed, my eyes going wide.

"Glad you like the idea of that as much as I do." He brushed his thumb across my cheek. "Soon, baby." Then he took a step away from me. "I gotta take a shower. Wouldn't want to get you covered in soot after you just cleaned up."

My pulse leaped at the thought of what his hands could do to get me dirty again. "Mm-hmm."

There was a knowing look in his eyes as he shrugged out of his leather vest and stripped out of his shirt. He gestured to the open bathroom door and smirked. "Unless you want to take another shower."

"Umm," I stuttered, shocked to find myself considering the suggestion even though we just met and barely knew each other. Not to mention how inexperienced I was with men.

My reaction to Pax was out of character for me, so it was probably good that he shook his head and gave me a small smile. "Get into bed, baby. We'll talk more in the morning."

"Okay."

I continued to gawk at him as he yanked the belt from his jeans and dropped it on the floor next to his boots. When he flicked open the snap on his jeans, I pressed my thighs together to ease the ache in my core. They rode low on his hips as he strode across the room, and with his back turned to me, I let my eyes eat up every inch of exposed skin.

My fingers itched to trace the black flames inked on his spine. Or the designs on his shoulders. The lettering on his forearm that I had noticed earlier, too.

He kicked the bathroom door shut behind him before I gave in to the temptation, and I wasn't sure if

I was relieved or disappointed that the opportunity had passed me by. At least my urge to be close to him was partially satisfied when I climbed into his bed and got under the covers because his woodsy masculine scent surrounded me.

Although I was comfortable and exhausted, I was too aware of Pax being naked in the shower to be able to fall asleep.

He was much faster in there than I'd been, most likely because it wasn't his first time trying to get soot off his tall, muscular body. Shaking my head at my one-track mind, I rolled over and pretended to be asleep when I heard him turn the doorknob. He hadn't taken any fresh clothes in there with him, so I wasn't surprised when he opened the dresser drawer, but that didn't mean it wasn't difficult not to turn around to sneak a peek at him...and his presumably bare butt.

It got even harder to act as though I was sleeping when I felt him slide into the bed next to me. He was only inches away from me and half-naked. I had on more clothes, but for some reason, I felt just as naked. It wasn't something I'd ever experienced before, and I had a feeling that I would enjoy it a whole lot more if I could actually see him.

My internal musings came to an abrupt halt

when Pax pulled me into his arms and brushed his lips against the crook of my neck. "I can hear your wheels turning from here, baby. Whatever you're thinking about so hard, we'll figure it out in the morning."

"Except now you gave me something else to think about," I whispered.

His breath was hot against my skin as he asked, "What's that?"

I gathered my courage and confessed, "I never thought my first kiss would be under circumstances like these."

"First kiss?" he echoed, rolling me over until I was flat on my back and he was hovering over me.

"Yeah."

My voice was almost inaudible, but it was enough to spur him into action. Cradling my cheek with his palm, he lowered his head until his lips brushed mine. Then he gave me a deep, wet kiss that was everything I'd ever dreamed of and more. His tongue swept between my lips to tangle with mine, stealing my breath. I gripped his shoulders and whimpered in protest when he pulled away. "After what you've been through tonight, now's not the time."

"It isn't?" I huffed.

"Nope." He yanked the blanket over my chest and positioned us so that we were on our sides with my back pressed against his chest. "Go to sleep before I give in to the temptation to do more."

I thought that was where this was headed since he was only in his boxers and obviously turned on, judging by the hard length nestled against my butt. I wiggled, and he groaned. "That's enough. I'm not gonna fuck you tonight, baby."

I probably should've been grateful that he wasn't the kind of guy to take advantage of my vulnerability, but I fell asleep feeling disappointed more than anything else.

8

BLAZE

I didn't know how the fuck I'd managed it, but I'd lasted all night long without sinking my hard-as-steel cock into Courtney's pussy. Even when she was wiggling her sweet little ass against my groin, I didn't give in. That should have won me a fucking medal.

Finding out that she was a virgin had fucked with my head. Knowing I was gonna get to pop that ripe cherry...to be the first and only man to slide inside her tight pussy... The Neanderthal I had no idea lived deep inside me came roaring to the surface, demanding I claim my woman. Shouting at me to do whatever it took to make sure she would always be mine. My determination to wait had almost completely crumbled last night.

Her virginity was the only thing holding me back

now. She deserved more than a quick fuck. And I didn't want her to let me inside her tight body because she was vulnerable from the events of the last two days. I wanted to make sure Courtney knew exactly what she was getting into before I fucked her, and that wouldn't have been possible last night.

But waking up with her black hair splayed all over my chest and her leg hiked over my aching cock...I didn't think I could resist any longer.

She was still, and her breathing was even, but I had a feeling she was no longer asleep. I looked down at her, and her eyes were still closed, but a smile slowly curved her lips. She was so fucking cute.

My amusement quickly faded when her fingers trailed up my chest and traced the lines of the tattoos on my shoulders, leaving a trail of fire in their wake.

"You need to stop moving," I growled, my voice raspy from sleep and the raging hard-on I was trying to ignore.

Her eyes were hazy when they opened, and she slowly blinked up at me. I hoped she'd be a good girl and do as she was told, but I quickly realized there was a lot of sass under the sweet and sexy.

She inhaled softly, pushing her tits into my chest, and then wiggled her hips, making my aching cock throb even more.

I cleared my throat, then gave her an admonishing look. "Courtney," I growled, a warning clear in my tone.

Heat bloomed on her cheeks, but she blinked innocently—too innocently. When her hips moved again, I grabbed them and slammed my mouth down on hers.

It was only meant to distract her, but the second our lips connected, I was lost. My tongue slid inside to rub with hers. Tasting. Savoring.

A sweet sight fell from her lips, and her fingers reached up to grip my hair, her body pressing even closer to mine.

I glided a hand down to her ass, cupping her plump cheek and groaning when her body heat practically burned me through the thin material of the boxers.

Moving swiftly, I rolled her onto her back and settled over her, snuggling my big, fat cock in the apex of her thighs. "I can't wait to feel this tight little pussy wrapped around my cock," I groaned against her lips.

When I rocked into her heat, she broke the kiss, and she looked up at me with swollen lips and wide eyes. "I thought you said no sex," she panted,

My lips curled up into a wicked smile. "I said I

wouldn't fuck you last night, baby. Never said anything about the morning."

"Oh?" she breathed, her hazel eyes heated. "What's changed?"

A stray strand of her long ebony hair was resting on her pale cheek, and I rubbed it between my fingers for a second before pushing it behind her ear. I met her gaze. "With everything that happened the last two days, I wanted to make sure you had a little time to adjust."

Her tongue swept against her bottom lip. "Adjust to what?"

"To the idea of being mine."

She quirked an eyebrow. "Yours?"

My cock twitched at her sassy smile, and a shiver wracked her body. "All fucking mine," I grunted.

"Do I get a say in this?" Her tone was teasing. So damn adorable.

"Nope," I replied, popping the p. "You agreed to be mine the second you let me climb into this bed and hold your delicious body against mine."

One of my hands was still on her ass, and I gently squeezed the cheek. "This ass is mine." I slid my hand around to the front and up to cup one of her perfect breasts. "These sexy as fuck tits are mine." I moved my hand up to her face and traced her lips. "This mouth is mine." Then I collared her neck for a moment before gliding my hand down, over her breast, down her stomach, and into the waistband of the boxers to cup her naked center.

Courtney froze, not even breathing.

"This pussy," I growled as I dipped my middle finger between her folds. She was drenched, making her slick so my digit easily pushed into her tight channel. She cried out and bucked her hips, inching me in a little farther.

My eyes locked with hers and I grunted, "This cherry. It's mine. All fucking mine, do you understand?"

Courtney's tits bounced with each panted breath, making my cock swell even more. "What—" She broke off into a moan when I swirled my finger inside her, then cleared her throat and rasped, "What does that mean exactly?"

Gently, I added a second finger, stretching her because if I didn't, my monster cock was gonna tear her in two.

"I'm the only one who is allowed inside this juicy pussy," I muttered. My eyes narrowed, and I pierced her with a warning look. "That includes you, baby."

"Me?" she gasped, her back arching as I scissored my digits.

"That's right, baby." I smirked at her. "I'm the only one who gets to make you come. You need a release, I will take care of you. This is *my* pussy."

Her cheeks reddened as she looked at my chest instead of meeting my eyes. "I've...ummm. I've never..."

Cocking my head to the side, I smiled tenderly. "You've never had an orgasm, baby?"

I fucking loved the idea of being the only fingers, mouth, and cock that would ever make her come.

"No," she whispered.

I groaned at her soft confession. My dick couldn't get any harder, but it pulsed, pressing firmly against her center, pushing my fingers just a little deeper. It was weeping pre-come and begging to be inside her.

"Gonna change that right now, baby," I murmured, pulling my hand from the boxers and gripping both sides of her hips. In a blink, I'd flipped our positions and settled her over the big bulge in my underwear.

Her legs straddled my hips and she sat up to look down at me. The T-shirt she was wearing covered most of her beautiful body, so I gripped the hem and slowly drew the soft material up until I could pull it over her head and toss it away.

"Holy fuck," I breathed as I took in the view. Her naked body was even more exquisite than I imagined. Her round, full tits were tipped with stiff, rosy peaks that were begging for my mouth. *Soon.*

"How does my cock feel between your legs?" I asked, moving her so my dick was snug against her core, making her eyes dilate until they were almost entirely black. My eyes dropped to where we were connected. The thin material of both boxers did nothing to contain my straining dick and didn't keep her heat from scorching my shaft.

Her cheeks heated, and she bit her lip before whispering, "You're, um...really big."

I chuckled, though the strain from holding back made the sound lack humor. "Flattery will only get you fucked raw, baby."

Bucking my hips, I smiled wickedly when she gasped and ground down on my cock.

"How do I feel between your legs now, baby?"

"Umm..." Her eyes twinkled, and she met my gaze. "It's okay."

Her sass made my cock twitch, and a bead of pre-come leaked from the tip again. "Just okay? Then we're definitely not doing this right."

"Show me," she breathed.

I captured her wrists and placed her palms on

my chest. Then I cupped her hips and guided her so she rubbed up and down on my dick.

"Pax," she moaned, her head dropping back.

"This pussy belongs to me, Courtney," I grunted, drawing her gaze back to my face. "Which means no getting off by yourself. But you can absolutely use me to fuck yourself, baby. In fact, it's highly encouraged."

Courtney looked a little uncertain, so I showed her again, then murmured. "Fuck my cock, baby. I want to see you use my dick to give you pleasure."

Her cheeks flushed, but she adjusted her sexy ass on top of me, then repeated the motions I'd shown her. "Oh, yes, Pax..." she moaned.

She stilled for a second, but when her glossy eyes met mine, and she saw the encouragement in them, her hips began to move in earnest. Her eyes shut as her fingers gripped my chest, using me for leverage while she humped my aching cock.

"That's it, baby." I slid my hands down to grip her ass but let her lead. "Grind on my cock, let the pressure build until you feel like you're going to break. Oh, fuck, baby. Your pussy is so hot. Keep going, do whatever feels good."

Her movements grew harsher and faster as the pleasure built. She gasped for air, her muscles grew taut, and her fingernails dug into the skin of my chest.

She was close. A part of me felt a little guilty for what I was about to do, but I'd meant it when I said her orgasms were mine.

Before she could find her release, I gripped her hips to stop her movements and flipped her over. Her eyes flew open as she landed with her back on the pillows, and I hovered over her.

"Hey," she pouted. "I was just getting to the really good part."

I grinned devilishly and shrugged. "Like I said... I'm the only one who gets to make you come."

She let out a surprised shriek when I growled and ripped the boxers off her body before tossing them over my shoulder.

Her pussy was perfect. Puffy lips, a juicy pink center, and a mouthwatering little pleasure button peeking out from beneath it's good.

Sliding one finger in, I felt her channel clench, and her legs fell open, giving me full access to her snug, virgin hole.

"So fucking tight," I murmured, swirling my finger inside her.

Leaning forward, I brushed my mouth against her clit, unable to resist sliding my tongue down her slit. She moaned, and her legs shook, her hips bucking up, seeking more.

"Fuck, baby," I grunted. "I've never tasted anything so delicious."

I wanted to drink down every last drop, so I hooked in another finger, pressing the perfect spot while I sucked hard.

Courtney gasped, and her hips began to pump in wild abandon. Her hands grasped the sides of my head as she fucked my face. Then she stilled before screaming as her pussy expanded and opened up for me while she came hard on my tongue.

I could have spent all day eating her incredible pussy, but my cock was done waiting, so I had to practically rip my mouth from her pulsing core before I crawled back up and took her swollen mouth in a deep kiss.

Pulling back, I stared down into her hazy eyes, clouded with passion, and come spurted from my dick. "You're so fucking gorgeous when you come, baby," I growled before I devoured her mouth again.

Her body was still trembling beneath me as she kissed me back with equal fervor.

Removing my hand from her center, I swirled my fingers around her pretty pink nipples, then sucked each one clean. I continued to stimulate her rosy tips while putting my hand back between her legs. I worked her pussy, stretching it and slowly adding fingers, trying to get her ready to take my big cock.

"Yes!" she cried, her hips undulating as I finger fucked her. "Pax! Oh, yes! Yes!"

She gripped my wrist between us, urging me to move harder and faster, urging me to just the right spot. I moved up to kiss her, and her moans filled my mouth. She was close, so I slowed my movements.

"Ready to take my cock?" I asked.

"Yes, Pax," she whimpered. "Make me yours."

"You're already mine," I growled.

I shucked my boxers, then settled back between her legs, just the head of my cock pressing against her pussy lips. "Spread those legs for me, baby."

She immediately obeyed, and I gave her a quick, appreciative kiss.

"I want you to watch," I murmured. "Look while my big cock fills your tight pussy."

Her eyes went to where we connected, and I slowly slid into her scorching-hot core. She was incredibly snug, and her body struggled to accept my thick girth.

It was another reminder that I was the first and only to be inside this sweet, untouched pussy. When

I felt resistance, I took her lips in a powerful kiss, hoping to distract her as I punched through her virginity.

Ripping my mouth away, I shouted, "Mine!" I kept pushing in, choosing to keep going until I was filling her completely before I gave her core a moment to adjust to my size. "You're doing so good, baby," I praised softly. She whimpered, and I kissed her again as I continued to move. "Just a little more. Relax, Courtney. That's it, good girl. I'm almost there."

"There's more?" she squeaked, making me drop my forehead to hers and chuckle. How in the fuck I was able to laugh at that moment was beyond me. It was just Courtney...she was so damn perfect.

"Just a little."

"That's what you said before," she muttered, her lips puffed into a cute little pout. But the pain in her eyes shredded me, so I was incredibly relieved when my hips finally met hers, my balls smacking against her ass as I bottomed out inside her pussy.

"You're amazing, baby," I breathed. "You did so good. I knew you could do it. Your body was made to take me. Damn, you feel good. Fuck."

Remaining still was torture, but I'd forced my

way in without a break, so I was determined to give her as much time as she needed to relax.

To my surprise, her nails raked down my back, and her thighs clenched around my hips. Her gaze was riveted to the spot where we were connected, and when I shallowly glided in and out, she watched the way our connected bodies moved together with her mouth creating a little O.

"That's so fucking hot," I rasped. "Your pussy is choking my cock like it's never gonna let go. Oh, fuck yeah...squeeze—fuck yes!"

She wrapped her legs around my waist, and I growled as I sank in so deep the tip of my cock bumped her cervix.

"Oh, Pax," Courtney panted. "Yes. Right there! Yes! Harder! YES!"

I gripped her hips and slammed her hips up every time I slammed into her viselike channel. My speed increased, and my movements became wild and frantic. Her inner walls were wrapped so fucking tight around my shaft. It was better than anything I'd ever felt in my life. I knew I wouldn't be able to hold back my release for very long. She needed to come again right now.

Sliding my thumb between us, I circled her

swollen clit, then rubbed it in the same rhythm I was pounding in and out of her slick heat.

Courtney gasped, gripping the sheets in clenched fists as she arched her body, taking in more of my cock. "That's it, baby. Oh fuck yes. Come, baby. I need you to let go for me. Come all over my big fat cock."

"Pax!" she screamed. Her whole body shook as she strangled my dick, her orgasm hitting hard and causing her inner muscles to ripple around my shaft, milking my climax from me.

I ran my hands over every inch of her beautiful body as I chased my pleasure inside her. My balls were tingling, but I wanted to come together.

"Give me one more, baby," I demanded as I reached for the last of my energy, fucking her so hard the mattress was squeaking loudly in protest. "Come for me again. Open up so I can fill you," I commanded, watching my cock plunge in and come out shiny with her release before she swallowed it up again.

The connection between us was so intense, her pussy so fucking hot, my cock scraping along her walls...it suddenly hit me that I was riding her bare. But the fleeting thought left as quickly as it had come.

The Neanderthal was in charge, and he was gonna make sure Courtney was mine irrevocably. I was gonna fuck her hard and often until she was growing our baby inside her.

As we neared the peak, our eyes locked, and her mouth opened in a silent cry. Her walls clamped down around me, and then her orgasm crashed over her. "Pax, yes! Oh yes!"

I exploded with a roar, and her tight little pussy milked every last drop I had to give her.

Courtney collapsed against the pillows, breathing hard as I rolled us so that she was sprawled on my chest, our bodies still connected.

I wanted nothing more than to stay exactly where I was, but I also knew my woman would be even more sore if I gave in to the impulse. It took everything I had to pull out of her warm pussy, cuddling her close when she murmured in protest. Grabbing a washcloth to clean between her legs could wait until she was ready for me to move.

9
COURTNEY

Being wrapped in Pax's arms after having two amazing orgasms was almost as good as the sex we'd just had. Waiting to give up my virginity to him had been more than worth it.

"Wow," I panted, resting my cheek against his broad chest.

"I'm gonna take that as confirmation I just proved why I'm the only one who gets in your pussy." His body shook beneath me as he chuckled. "'Cause I sure as fuck know what to do with it."

I laughed softly. "I can't really argue with that logic."

"Not after you just finished screaming my name." His arms tightened around me. "Which is why I wanted you to call me Pax, not Blaze."

I tilted my head back to smile at him. "It's kinda funny that you want me to use your real name, especially during sex, while I really like hearing you call me baby."

My stomach rumbled, the sound loud enough to echo around the room, making Pax chuckle. "Hungry, baby?"

"Yeah, I haven't really eaten much since my run-in with those guys, and I skipped dinner last night." I beamed a satisfied smile at him. "Plus, we just burned off a ton of calories."

He slid off the mattress, taking me with him. "Then I better feed you extra so we can get in another workout when you're ready to take me again."

"Are you going to impress me with your cooking skills?" I asked as my body slid down his before my toes touched the floor.

"Nah, I think I've already shown off for you enough for one morning." He wrapped my hair around his fist and tugged my head back, devouring my mouth in a deep kiss that left me wanting more. "I'll save my next display of skills for when we're back in bed."

I blinked up at him, shaking my head to dispel

the sensual fog his kiss had put me in. "Sounds like an excellent plan to me."

He patted my butt. "Go get cleaned up, and I'll find something for you to wear."

I did a decent job untangling my hair with my fingers and used an extra toothbrush I found under the sink, but I was swimming in the clothes Pax gave me. There wasn't anything I could do about it, though. I didn't even have my purse or...

"Oh crap."

Pax stepped out of the bathroom, where he'd been getting ready after I finished. "What's wrong?"

"My car is parked on the backside of the warehouse, right next to the fence. I locked it, but my purse is inside the trunk. I hope nobody broke into it."

"Like you did with the warehouse?" he teased with a grin, pulling his cell phone out of his pocket.

"You're going to hold that over my head forever, aren't you?" I grumbled.

My cheeks filled with heat when I realized how that sounded...as though I expected us to be together for a long time. Although Pax had called me his plenty of times while we were having sex, that could've just been in the heat of the moment.

Luckily, he didn't seem to notice that I was feeling awkward about what I'd just said.

"Probably." He tapped his finger against his screen and then looked up at me with a smile. "Gimme your keys. One of the prospects is going to grab your car."

"That'd be great." I dug through the pockets of my ruined pants and fished out my keys.

As soon as I handed them to him, there was a knock on the door. Pax strode over and opened it just enough to hand them to a guy in the hallway.

"Be careful with it," he warned.

"Of course, Blaze."

When he shut the door and turned back to me, my brows were raised. "That was fast."

"Damn straight," he agreed with a nod. "We screen the fuck out of our prospects and only take the guys who're willing to work hard to patch in."

"And working hard includes driving across town to fetch my car?" I asked, intrigued by how that interaction had gone.

Wrapping his arm around my waist, Pax tugged me close. "It includes anything I ask a prospect to do."

"Look at you, already impressing me again, and

we aren't even back in bed yet," I murmured, stroking my palms up his chest.

"I'll show you something truly impressive." He dashed my hopes when he added, "After I feed you."

I felt a little awkward as Pax led me downstairs, but I took comfort in having him by my side. Although we had only known each other for half a day, he had already earned my complete trust.

Hanging around bikers in a motorcycle clubhouse might not have been something I would have pictured myself doing before I met him, but I couldn't imagine he would be part of a club filled with bad guys. Especially after what he told me about how careful they were with new members.

Nothing could've prepared me for what we found when we reached the kitchen.

Several of the guys who'd been in the clubhouse when Pax carried me inside were standing in a semicircle around an obviously pregnant woman. There was a man on his knees in front of her, his palm pressed against her rounded belly. "Doesn't feel like a Braxton Hicks to me, Stella."

If she was the woman Pax had mentioned last night, then he must be the club president, King. Seeing him literally on his knees for his woman confirmed what I'd been thinking about the men of the Hounds of Hellfire...they weren't anything like the stereotypes shown on television shows—except for being big, hot, and scary.

"I don't know what to tell you." Stella shrugged with a sigh. "They're still irregular and sometimes go completely away, like when I sit this way."

She carefully lowered herself onto the nearest chair, crossing her ankles and shifting so that she was mostly sitting on her right butt cheek.

A muscle in King's jaw jumped as he stared down at her. "Then stay exactly the fuck like that."

"Absolutely not." She slowly stood again and planted her fists on her hips. "I am more than ready to get this baby out of me. I feel like I've been pregnant forever. If sitting in a weird position is going to up my odds of going into real labor, then I'm going to do it."

Pax pulled me against his side, his head dipping low as he murmured, "Hope you're not like this when you're pregnant. Your kinda sassy is cute, but I'd probably drive myself up the wall trying to figure out how to give you what you want. And it's not like you can rush shit like this. Babies are born when they're ready."

"Actually, there are things you can do to help

induce labor naturally," I corrected, drawing everyone's attention to me.

Stella shrieked, "Please tell me you have a list. I'm desperate enough to try just about anything. If you have an idea that'll kick start my labor, I swear we'll be best friends for life."

I got a little tongue-tied with everyone staring at me, so it took a moment to gather my thoughts before I answered, "Umm, one of my coworkers mentioned a few things. Spicy food, acupuncture, and ah...sex."

"I know which one I vote for," King rumbled.

Stella rolled her eyes. "We all do, but what you're actually going to do is find me some spicy food."

"Whatever you want, baby." He gave her a quick kiss before turning to the guy to his right. "Check to see if there's any salsa in the pantry, Echo."

"Will do," he agreed before striding away.

"I think she also mentioned pineapple," I added.

"Ooh, pineapple." She rubbed her hands together. "That sounds delicious."

"Doubt we got one of those," another of the guys grumbled, shaking his head.

King glared at him. "Thought you were resourceful, Wizard."

"I'll get a whole damn box of pineapples

dropped off ASAP," he promised, grabbing a tablet off the nearest table and tapping on the screen.

It turned out that my suggestions and his effort weren't necessary because Stella suddenly clutched her rounded belly with a gasp as fluid dripped onto the floor between her feet. "I think my water just broke."

"Fuck, I gotta get you to the hospital." King carefully lifted her into his arms as he ordered, "Bring your truck to the front, Onyx. I'm not gonna drive while my woman is in labor. I'll stay in the back with her while you get us there."

"You got it, Prez."

I stared while he stalked out of the kitchen with Stella in his arms and Onyx right behind him. Then I turned to Pax. "Life in your clubhouse is a lot more exciting than I expected, and that's saying a lot."

"First time we've had an old lady go into labor in the clubhouse as far as I know, and I've been a member for almost two decades."

"Two decades?" I echoed, tilting my head. "How old are you?"

Joining in on my teasing, the other guy who hadn't said anything yet chimed in, "Yeah, grandpa. How old are you?"

"Shut up, Ink," Blaze grumbled. "Doesn't matter

that you've been patched in, I'll still kick your ass to demonstrate exactly how young I am."

"Don't worry, Pax." I winked at him. "You already proved yourself to me."

That shut down his friends, and they mostly left us alone while I whipped together some pancakes and bacon. Except to beg for food, so I made extra. Then Pax made them clean everything up while he took me back to his room to burn off the calories we'd just consumed.

10

BLAZE

"Take it you're officially a dad?" I asked with a grin when I answered my cell, putting it on speakerphone and setting it on my desk. King was at the hospital with his old lady, so I assumed he was calling with the good news.

"Fuck yeah, I am," he crowed.

I chuckled at his smug tone. "Boy or girl?"

"Boy. Cadell Connor Kingsley. Twenty-two inches, ten pounds."

Wincing, I mumbled, "Ouch. Ten? Stella doing okay?"

King's wife was tiny, so that couldn't have been easy.

"She was a fucking champ."

"You call Pierce?" King and I were still close to the former prez. Despite being closer to the age of my grandfather, he'd been more of a father to me than mine ever had. And King had bounced around the foster system, so Pierce was pretty much the only father figure he'd ever had.

"Yeah," he confirmed, a smile clear in his voice. "He was at the Silver Saints clubhouse, so he had to stop and tell every person who walked by during our conversation."

"Proud grandpa," I laughed.

"Told me to tell you he wants more babies to spoil, so get to it."

I grinned and thought about how I'd spent the morning with my woman. "Working on it."

"Guessing you need me to order a vest?"

"Already called the company and put in a bulk order," I informed him, making him chuckle. "We'll have a stash, just in case. Then all they will need is the names stitched onto them."

"Prime example why you're my VP."

His tone was almost jolly, and it was freaking me out.

"How long is this chipper attitude going to last?"

"Chipper? When did you turn seventy?"

Rolling my eyes, I opened a folder from the stack next to me. "Get back to your family. I have shit to do."

"Sure," he agreed. "Call if you need anything."

"Consider yourself on paternity leave, Prez. I have things handled."

"Excellent. I'll let you know when we're home so you can come and meet your godson."

With King at the hospital, I was covering all the club shit. Plus, I didn't want Courtney away from the clubhouse and wasn't willing to leave her unless it was to deal with the threat looming over her. So we decided that I'd wait to see them until they came back, rather than go to the hospital.

"Looking forward to it."

After hanging up, I began reading through the profiles of possible clients that Ash had dropped off.

"Found her, Blaze."

My head lifted from the document I was reading, and I stared hard at Ink as he strolled into my office and came to a stop in front of my desk.

"My cousin Raffaele called." Ink was Nic DeLuca's cousin, the head of the DeLuca crime family. His older brother, Enzo, was Nic's second in command. Ink and his mother had moved south to get away from the Mafia, and they'd settled in Georgia because his aunt was married to our former prez, Pierce.

Ink—whose real name was Matteo DeLuca but was given the road name Ink because he was an extremely talented tattoo artist—had become friends with Onyx, who managed our tattoo shop, Hellbound Studio. They were both amazing and had long waitlists.

Ink didn't have anything to do with Mafia business, but he stayed in touch with his relations, including Raffaele...who was the head of The Family in the south.

When we first contacted him, he'd found where they'd replaced Sabrina in their files. But when we sent people to retrieve her, we found that she'd taken off, so no one, not even the Hounds or the Mafia, knew where she was.

Wizard had been on the money trail, collaborating with some of Raffaele's guys who were also deep in the tech business.

"Lilianna managed to find security footage that showed the last time Sabrina was in Biloxi. Paid with cash for the first few days, but Wizard was still able to get a general idea of her movements. She used a card yesterday, though. Must have run out and couldn't get to a bank."

"Picked up and on her way back here?" I confirmed.

Ink nodded as he shoved his hands into the pockets of his jeans. "She's been tight-lipped about the rest of the money, but Wizard says he thinks most of it is still in the bank account that's under her new identity."

"How much is most?" Since Courtney's attackers had been vague when they confronted her, we didn't have any idea how much money Sabrina had stolen.

"From tracking all the deposits and withdrawals, and factoring in what she paid us, Wizard thinks she might owe them about thirty grand."

"Thirty? The bitch stole thirty grand from a drug kingpin?" I shouted. Sabrina was clearly off her fucking rocker.

No wonder the men were threatening Courtney. If I were a lesser man, I would have given the order for my guys to deliver Sabrina straight to the enemy for putting my woman in so much danger. But feeding Sabrina to the wolves would make me a villain too, and my soul was already black enough. I didn't want it tarnished to the point where Courtney couldn't see beyond the darkness to how she lit up my heart.

"She give up the name of the head of the organization?"

"No, but I found him," Wizard announced from the doorway. "Set up a meet for tomorrow morning."

I grunted with approval. "Good. Get what you can from Sabrina, then let me know how much we're short, and I'll get the money." Luckily, my jobs and smart investments had made me a very wealthy man.

Wizard shook his head. "King specifically told me to make sure the club handled the missing money. We took her on as a client, so he's taking responsibility."

"Bullshit," I argued in a bellow. "Courtney is mine. I'll take care of it."

Ink backed up a few steps, watching me warily.

I was a very patient man and rarely lost my temper, so I understood his hesitancy. But when it came to my woman, I'd burn the fucking world down to keep her safe.

"It's already done," Wizard murmured, crossing his arms over his chest. "Talked to King on the way here."

"While he was with his old lady and newborn son?" I growled.

"He called me."

Of course he did.

"Fine," I snapped. "Somebody just get me the fucking money and send me a dossier on the men I'm meeting with tomorrow."

"Check your email," Wizard said, lifting his chin in the direction of my computer.

I nodded. "Not a word to Courtney. I'm gonna tell her after I read through the info."

Both men agreed, then left me to do my research.

When I was familiar enough with the players to feel like I had an advantage in the game for the next day, I shut everything down and went to find Courtney.

She'd mentioned puttering around in the kitchen, but when I walked through the door into the spacious room, I wasn't expecting the scene before me.

The large island in the center of the cooking area was currently covered with containers of treats.

Courtney was bent over the oven, giving me a fantastic view of her heart-shaped ass. Then she stood, holding a metal sheet in her mittened hands, and turned around. The smell of cinnamon and chocolate invaded my nose, and the delicious spread almost sidetracked me.

As she set the tray on the counter, she looked up and saw me. A beautiful smile lit her face, making my chest warm and my heart beat a little faster.

"Hi," she said softly.

"Hey, baby." I held out my hand and beckoned for her to come to me. "I have news."

11

COURTNEY

Relief washed over me as his words registered in my brain.

They found Sabrina.

"Oh my gosh. I can't believe you managed it this quickly."

He smirked at me with a quirked brow. "Almost sounds as though you were lying about how impressive you thought I was."

"Of course not." I rolled my eyes. "It's just that I'm so excited all of this might actually be over soon."

Pax's grin disappeared as he yanked me against his chest. "I better not be part of that all you're talkin' about, baby. Because we're not gonna be fucking over."

"I definitely didn't mean you."

He brushed his lips against mine in a kiss that left me wanting more. "Good."

I wasn't sure if I was more relieved to hear that they knew where Sabrina was or that Pax still wanted to be together after those guys were no longer a threat to me. Either way, the tears welling in my eyes started to flow down my cheeks.

"Hey, baby, don't cry." He wiped his thumb across my cheek, swiping away the tears.

I sniffled, doing my best to get my emotions under control, but it was hard. "I can't help it. I just… there's been a lot of highs and lows in such a short time."

"I'm assuming I'm one of the highs?" he asked, pressing a kiss to my forehead.

"The highest of highs," I confirmed with a watery smile.

"C'mon, let's head to my room. Give you a little more privacy."

He led me out of the kitchen—where I'd been stress baking, much to his club brothers' delight. Our fingers were intertwined as he led me to his room, kicking the door shut behind us. I padded over to the bed and sat down, tears springing from my eyes again as another wave of relief crashed over me.

Pax knelt in front of me, his hands shaking as he

placed them on my knees. "Thought I told you not to cry."

I inhaled deeply, then let out my breath slowly as I met his gaze. "These are happy tears, Pax. I'm just…I'm so relieved that my life will finally go back to normal. Even if it's a new one because you're in it now."

He laughed as he wiped the tears from my cheeks. "And it'll be a much better one with me around."

There was no denying that. Although I'd been through hell because of the stunt Sabrina pulled, in a weird kind of way, I felt as though I owed her because I never would've met Pax otherwise. "It will."

"Good because there's no going back now that I've had you. I meant it when I told you that you were mine, and I guess now I'll have to prove it."

Before I could respond, he leaned forward and his lips crushed to mine, taking all the breath from my lungs. When his tongue slid into my mouth, I melted into him, wrapping my arms around his neck to pull him down to the bed with me. Something that I knew darn well only worked because he went along with it.

Pax was so much bigger than me, but he fit

perfectly against my body as I spread my legs to give him space to settle between them. His dick was already hard, and I could feel it pressing against my core even through both of our jeans.

I didn't even realize I was rubbing myself against him to feel some friction until he broke our kiss. "I'm in control, baby. Be patient, and I'll give you what you need."

He followed up his promise by sliding his hand between us to cup my pussy. His touch only eased some of the ache, and I wanted more. Needed it since I'd quickly become addicted to the pleasure only this man could give me.

"Please, Pax," I managed to pant.

He laughed again, his breath hot on my lips. "Love how responsive you are to me, and only me. So needy. But I have to get you warmed up before you take my big cock."

I pressed my head back against the pillows as he slid down the length of my body, a wicked smile on his gorgeous face as he yanked off my jeans and panties and tossed them to the side.

He'd already seen, touched, and tasted every inch of me, so there was no hint of embarrassment at being laid bare in front of him. Only desire coursed through my veins when his heated gaze zeroed in on my pussy, heat simmering low in my belly.

He spread my legs farther before his rough tongue slid over my slit. Just that slight, wet touch had me shivering with anticipation. He'd trained my body to know what was coming next...so much pleasure.

He added a finger inside me, and my body stretched to fit him as though some part of him was always meant to be there. And when he added his tongue again, using long strokes as he swirled his thick digit, my body tightened as my release started to build.

Gripping the sheets, I moaned, feeling the heat now bursting through my belly as my orgasm hit hard and fast. Bucking my hips, I met his eager mouth, now wet with my arousal, as he used his fingers and tongue to work me through my release.

"That's it, baby. Ride my face as you come, and give me another while you're at it," Pax growled before sucking hard on my clit.

Pleasure exploded behind my eyelids, taking me higher than I'd already been. My whole body shook as my second orgasm hit even harder than the first.

"Good girl," he praised, kneeling to quickly

shuck off his clothes, giving me the perfect view of his toned, naked body as he hovered over me.

I stroked my hand up one of his arms to trace the black ink that my tongue had licked over several times now.

Instead of sliding his hard ridges against my body like I wanted, he reached down to rip my shirt, the fabric tearing in half before he tossed it aside.

"Pax," I gasped.

He grinned, making quick work of discarding my bra too. "I'll buy you a new one. But I had to get my mouth on your perfect tits right the fuck now."

He dipped his head and licked my puckered nipple, then trailed his tongue along my skin to the other.

I whimpered as he lightly nibbled at my sensitive skin.

"You like that, baby?" he murmured, his mouth still against me.

I nodded because words weren't able to come out of my throat since all of my breath was caught in my chest.

He continued to suck on my nipples, alternating to give them equal attention. Then his fingers slid between us, dipping right back into my soaked pussy.

It felt incredible, like always, and I moaned,

already feeling the pressure build again between my thighs. I bucked my hips closer, desperate to come again, but he abruptly pulled his fingers out of me.

"Noooo," I cried, reaching out for him.

"Told you that I'd give you what you want, baby. But you're not gonna take it, except for when I tell you that you can," he chided, his eyes burning into mine. "Remember, I own this pussy. I'm the only one who gets to make it come."

"I know," I whispered, dropping my hands at my sides as I got even wetter at his possessive tone. His alphaness didn't turn me off. It only made me want him more.

"Good girl."

He rewarded me by finally sliding his dick inside me.

Each inch he gave me sent a burst of pleasure directly to my womb. I could barely contain my shivering as I gripped his shoulders, needing something to hold on to while I felt as though I was going to fly apart.

"My fucking pussy," he growled, pushing his hips to drive into me over and over again. "All fucking mine."

"Yes, oh yes," I cried, lifting to meet each of his thrusts.

I gripped his shoulders harder, my nails digging into his flesh as he groaned out my name. "Courtney, fuck yeah. You're so close, your pussy is already starting to milk my cock. Gonna fill you all the way with my come."

I should've been worried about the potential consequences of him taking me without anything between us, but all I could focus on was the pleasure he was giving me. And the dream I had last night of a beautiful baby boy with his dark hair and gray eyes.

So I urged him on by murmuring, "Yes, fill me up, Pax. Mark me inside and out as yours."

"That's it, baby. Come again all over my cock before I fill you with my seed." He added his thumb to my clit and rubbed in the same motion he pounded into me.

His deep growl mixed with the pleasure of him thrusting inside me and had my orgasm coming even harder than the other two before it. I saw stars and felt a wave of heat flood through me as it crashed over me.

"Fuck yes," he groaned, pumping into me three more times before I felt the hot splash of his release against my inner walls.

Pax collapsed against me, careful not to give me too much of his weight as he peppered kisses across my sweaty collarbone and neck. I couldn't move. My entire body was boneless after all that pleasure.

I didn't know how long we lay there, the beating of our hearts in sync, before Pax lifted his head. "As much as I want to stay here with you, we need to clean up. Then I gotta get to work on making sure those assholes stay the fuck away from you now that we found Sabrina."

"Another of your plans that I can happily get behind."

12

BLAZE

"You're Sabrina, I'm guessing?" I muttered as I sauntered into the room where we were holding her.

The land our compound sat on was pretty big, but Pierce hadn't wanted the building where people were questioned to be near his daughter.

So one of the warehouses the club owned just up the road—with paperwork buried so deep in shell companies that not even the CIA could connect it to us, thanks to our prez being a former operative—was used for more intense interrogation, weapons storage, and other things that pertained to some less than legal activities.

"Who are you?" she asked, her voice quivering with fear.

"Relax. I'm not going to hurt you."

"Probably," Kevlar grunted, twirling a knife through his fingers. Some people might have assumed he was just trying to be intimidating, but truthfully, Kevlar was a little unhinged. He was the kind of guy who liked to play Five Finger Fillet.

I shot him a warning glance when Sabrina paled.

Kevlar shrugged and tossed the knife onto a nearby table. It was the only furniture in the room besides two chairs.

Sabrina was cuffed to one, and I flipped the other around to straddle it, facing her.

"You've really pissed off the wrong people, Sabrina," I said conversationally.

"If you hadn't tracked me down, they'd never have found me," she whined.

"You're right. We're fucking good at what we do. Problem is, you've pissed us off, too."

Sabrina shook her head frantically. "I don't know what you're talking about. I paid for your services."

I cocked my head to the side and studied her for a second. "You really think we wouldn't figure out that you paid us with dirty money?"

She flinched and squirmed in her seat uncomfortably. "Does it really matter where the cash came from?"

"Obviously, you didn't do your research when it came to the Hounds of Hellfire. We have a fucking code, Sabrina." My expression twisted with disgust. "It's not just about the dirty money. It's about the fact that you left your roommate to pay the price for your sins."

Sabrina winced and said softly, "I didn't think they would go after her."

I shot to my feet and stalked over to her, bending down to put my hands on the armrests. She clearly saw how close I was to the edge because she reared back as far as she could, and her eyes swam with terror.

"Yes, you fucking did. You just didn't give a shit. But it's your damn lucky day, bitch. All I care about is making sure that Courtney is safe. So you're gonna tell me where the rest of the money is. If you do, without needing to be convinced, then you'll be free to leave."

"You won't tell them where to find me?"

I shoved away from the chair and stood back, my feet braced apart and my arms crossed over my chest. "No."

She hesitated, glancing between Kevlar and me, then tears filled her eyes. "I'm so sorry. I spent it—"

"Do NOT fucking lie to me, woman," I snarled.

Sabrina flinched again, then whispered, "What I didn't put in my account is in a safety deposit box."

She gave us the address, and I shot Kevlar a meaningful look. He pulled out his phone and sent a text while I turned back to Sabrina.

I questioned her for a few more minutes, then told Kevlar to have someone take her to the airport.

When I returned to my office, several of my brothers were waiting for me. We went over plans for the meeting the following morning, then I retrieved my woman and spent the night inside her sweet pussy.

"Who the fuck are you?" a greasy guy in ratty jeans and a dirty hoody muttered when he answered the door at the stash house.

"Blaze," I grunted.

The man's beady eyes dropped to my vest, and I saw the flicker of fear in his eyes before he managed to hide it behind an insolent expression. "You're a Hounds of Hellfire?" he asked, looking from me to the enforcers, Rebel and Ink, who stood directly behind me.

I scowled and snarled, "Think that's pretty

fucking obvious, asshole. So if you're smart, you'll get the fuck outta my way."

"Yo, Leon!" someone yelled from inside. "Shut the fucking door!"

"I don't know what you're doing here, but you need to leave," Leon insisted, trying to sound confident and demanding.

The pipsqueak couldn't keep up the act when I slapped my hand on the door to hold it open. "Lucky for you, I'm not staying. But these two"—I jerked my head back toward my brothers—"are gonna keep you guys company while I take care of some business with your boss."

I didn't wait for a response, just pivoted around and stomped down the stairs, muttering to my brothers, "If you don't hear from me in half an hour, burn the place down. With everyone in it."

Fifteen minutes later, I pulled my bike up to the front gate of a mansion in the wealthiest neighborhood in our county.

"Pax Driscoll," I told the security guard. He checked his log, then opened the gate and waved me through.

The road was a large circle drive in front of the house, and I pulled up and parked my bike off to the side by the front door.

When I rang the bell, an older man in a suit opened the door with a sour expression that looked like it might be permanent.

"May I help you?"

"I have an appointment with Trenton."

"Ah, yes. Do follow me."

He spun around and marched into the house, leaving me to shake my head in disbelief. I didn't think guys like him existed outside the movies.

He led me through an opulent lobby full of priceless antiques and shiny marble before stopping at a set of double doors made of thick, dark oak.

After a quick rap of his knuckles, he pulled open one of the doors and gestured for me to enter.

"Blaze, I presume." The man who spoke was sitting in a tall, sing-back chair near a giant fireplace that was blazing brightly. His clothes were clearly very expensive, and diamonds winked from his ears, around his neck, and on his pinky.

Again, I had the feeling I'd just walked onto a fucking movie set.

"Trenton?"

"Have a seat."

He waited for me to walk over and sit in the chair opposite him. "What can I do for you? Nic DeLuca was quite insistent that I take this meeting."

"I'm here to talk about Courtney Cartwright."

Trenton raised an eyebrow. "I sincerely hope she sent you to give me the location of her friend. I'd hate to have to send my men to convince her."

Rage exploded inside me, and before he could blink, I was on my feet, my gun pointed at his head.

"Don't. Ever. Threaten. Her. Again," I seethed.

My finger itched to pull the trigger. If I knew for sure that Trenton was the top of the food chain, he'd already be dead. But I didn't know if he answered to someone else.

Trenton glanced at the door, and I growled, "You really think I would come here without doing my homework, motherfucker? My guys neutralized your security the second I was through the gate."

The door to the office swung open, and Kevlar and Ace strolled in, followed by a few more enforcers, Tomcat, Cruz, and Falcon.

Ace carried a satchel, and he tossed it at Trenton's feet.

"That's thirty-five thousand. We're square. Sabrina and Courtney are no longer your concern."

Trenton eyed the bag greedily, but the jackass still asked, "And the product?"

We'd been thorough in our research, so I was

prepared for this question. "I suggest you take a closer look at your own."

"Jason?" Trenton asked, his brow furrowing.

I snorted. "That asshole's spine is as limp as his dick. Talking about the thugs who threatened Courtney."

His expression was dubious. "My men are—"

Tomcat handed me a folded piece of paper, and Trenton stopped talking.

"Check out this address."

Trenton outstretched his hand, but I held the paper just out of reach. "If anything happens to Courtney—if I even see any of your people within a hundred yards of her—I will burn every single one of your stash houses and storage warehouses to the ground. Then I'll put a bullet between your eyes and leave your body in the flames. And the guys who you sent to threaten her? Don't be surprised when the one who dared to touch her goes missing."

He frowned at me for a few seconds, then nodded and shook his hand a little.

After staring him down for another minute, I let him take the paper from me.

Then I flicked the safety on and returned my gun to the back of my jeans.

"We're done here."

13
COURTNEY

I had just pulled a batch of chocolate chip cookies out of the oven when Ash poked his head into the kitchen. "Your man just pulled through the gates."

He hadn't been gone long, but I was relieved when he returned to the compound. Not because that meant I had nothing to worry about anymore—I was just happy that Pax had come back safely to me.

I knew he and his club brothers could more than take care of themselves, but that didn't stop me from worrying about the man that I loved.

We hadn't shared that particular four-letter word with each other yet, but I had admitted to myself that I had fallen head over heels in love with Pax. Something that I planned to share with him soon.

"Thanks." I beamed a smile at Ash. "Feel free to take as many cookies as you want."

"No need for all that gratitude when all I did was take a minute to find you exactly where I knew you'd be." He patted his flat stomach. "But I sure as fuck am gonna still take you up on the offer."

I flashed him another grin as I hurried past him, dusting my hands off on my jeans. When I got halfway through the big recreational area next to the bar, Pax walked through the door. Seeing him, I picked up speed, throwing myself into his waiting arms when I got close enough.

"You're back," I cried, burying my face against his chest and breathing deeply. There was nothing better than feeling Pax's arms around me...except having his dick inside me. But that was a thought for later when we were alone in his room.

"I am, baby." His hold on me tightened before he stepped back to grin down at me. "It's all taken care of. You don't have anything to worry about anymore."

"Did you have to give Sabrina up to them?" Whatever fondness I might've felt for my roommate was long gone, but I still wouldn't want anything horrible to happen to her. That didn't stop me from wishing she'd step on a bunch of Legos. Or every time she ate pizza, which was her favorite, it would burn the roof of her mouth.

"No, that's not what we do. She might've made shit choices, but she doesn't deserve to pay with her life...or worse."

No wonder I fell in love with him so quickly.

Those three little words were on the tip of my tongue when Echo walked into the clubhouse, drawing Pax's attention away from me.

"Didn't expect to see you around today. Thought you were gonna be busy with that"—the look Pax shot my way let me know that he was choosing his words carefully, most likely because whatever Echo was supposed to be doing was club business—"situation you were handling."

"Had to come in and grab some shit because I'm moving in with my woman today," he explained.

"Your woman?" Pax echoed, asking the question that was on the tip of my tongue.

"Long story, man." Echo slapped him on the back. "But don't worry, she's not gonna interfere with what I have to get done. In fact, it's the opposite."

I still had no idea what they were discussing, but Pax seemed satisfied with his answer as he walked away.

When Echo was out of earshot, I asked, "That

was weird, right? And not just because you had to talk in code around me."

He shrugged with a deep chuckle. "Definitely unexpected, but after all the shit he's given King and me over finding our old ladies, it's about damn time that he finds the woman who's gonna knock him on his ass the same way you did with me."

"Old lady?" I whispered, my eyes widening.

"Damn straight," he growled, pulling me close.

"But I don't have a vest like Stella," I pointed out.

"Doesn't make you any less mine. Think I've already more than proved that to you," he argued. "But if it makes you feel better, your property patch is due to arrive any day now."

"Really?" I squealed, pressing trembling fingertips against my lips.

"I would've had it sooner if we had a system in place like the Silver Saints, a club that we have close ties with," he explained, shaking his head with an apologetic smile. "But most of the guys around here haven't found their women yet, so it hasn't really been an issue for us until recently."

"I look forward to wearing it proudly whenever it gets here."

His eyes heated to the color of molten steel. "I'll see if I can put a rush on it. Can't wait to see you model my property patch for me. Naked, in our bed."

"Maybe I should call in sick to work again tomorrow even though it's safe for me now," I suggested, wagging my brows. "Give us some time to practice for when my vest gets here."

I hadn't been back to the bank—or gone anywhere else off the Hounds of Hellfire compound—since Pax had brought me here after the fire. Luckily, I had plenty of paid time off saved up since I rarely took a sick or vacation day. And since I'd been so reliable for the past two years, my boss hadn't questioned me being out. Just wished for a speedy recovery while reassuring me that my shifts would be covered.

"Don't need to twist my arm to get me to agree to that plan," he murmured with a heated look in his gray orbs. "Hate the idea of you not being here all the time. Already got used to it."

"Same."

"Good because I was hoping you'd like the idea of moving in with me while we figure out something more permanent than my quarters here."

My eyes widened at his suggestion. "You want me to live with you?"

"Of fucking course," he growled. "You're my

woman, Courtney. You'll officially be my old lady as soon as your property patch gets here. I'm also gonna make you my wife and the mother of my kids. Where else would you live?"

"I can't think of anywhere else I'd rather be," I replied with a happy sigh.

"That's my good girl, giving me exactly what I want and need," he rasped. "I love you so damn much."

"I love you, too," I sniffled.

"You better, baby. Because you're never getting rid of me. We're gonna spend every day for the rest of our very long lives together."

I flashed him a watery smile that quickly turned into a thrilled gasp when King and Stella came through the doors, their newborn nestled in a carrier that he carefully carried in a big fist. Luckily, we were nearest to the entrance, so we beat everyone else to them.

Peering down at the sleeping baby, I sighed. "Oh my gosh. He is so cute."

"And fucking tiny," Pax added, sliding his arm around my shoulders as he got a good look at Cadell. "I thought a ten-pound baby would be bigger."

Stella glared at him. "Trust me, he's plenty big enough. If he'd weighed even one ounce more, I'm not sure I would've been able to give birth to him naturally."

"You did great, baby," King praised her with a proud smile.

"You're just saying that because I threatened to cut off your balls so you'd never be able to knock me up again right after I delivered your giant baby," she grumbled.

"Nah," he denied, shaking his head with a laugh. "I said the same thing before that, and you've already mentioned him needing another sibling even though he's only a couple of days old."

"Whatever."

We were bumped out of the way as the other Hounds of Hellfire squeezed in to meet their president's son.

"That will be us soon," Pax whispered against my ear.

"I hope so."

The past several days had been a whirlwind, but now that the danger had passed, I was beyond ready to start building a life—and family—with my white knight in black leather.

EPILOGUE
BLAZE

After what felt like the longest nine months of my life—but also the happiest—I was finally a dad. And I was going to be a fuck of a lot better one than mine had been. That was a promise I made to myself, my wife, and our barely-minutes-old son as I stared down at him.

"He's perfect," Courtney whispered.

"He is." Brushing a kiss against her damp brow, I murmured, "And you've never been more beautiful."

"Liar." She shook her head with a tired laugh.

It'd been a long twenty-five hours giving birth to him, but she'd come through it like a fucking pro. "I'm not lying. Not even a little. I'm in awe of you, baby."

"As you should be." She beamed a smile at me, a hint of sass in her exhausted eyes. "I worked hard to give you our little bundle of joy."

"No denying that." I cupped the back of his tiny head with my palm. "Hard to believe someone so small could cause so much trouble."

"You're telling me." She snorted and shook her head. "And I can't even complain too much since he weighs almost three pounds less than Cadell. I have no idea how Stella managed it, but I'm grateful you didn't give me a giant-headed baby to push out like King did to her."

I winked at her. "You're welcome."

There was a knock on the door, and then the nurse who'd helped during the labor and delivery peeked her head into the room. "Ready for visitors? You have a ton out in the waiting room."

I turned to Courtney. "Up to you, baby. You did all of the hard work. I was just here to hold your hand."

"Aw," the nurse cried, pressing her hand to her chest. "How is it that the toughest-looking ones are always the biggest marshmallows on the inside?"

"Don't let anyone else hear you call me that," I grumbled.

"Marshmallow." Courtney giggled before nodding at the nurse.

"Who would you like to start with?" she asked.

"My brother, please." My wife glanced up at me. "As long as that's okay with you. I'm not sure how long he can stay, and I want him to get as much time with his nephew as he can."

"Whatever you want, baby."

She beamed a bright smile at the nurse. "Definitely my brother."

The woman disappeared from the doorway, quickly replaced by my brother-in-law. He strode over to the other side of the bed, dropping onto the chair next to it before leaning in to give his sister a kiss on the cheek.

"Congratulations, Courtney." He glanced at me with a smile. "You too, Blaze."

At first, he hadn't been thrilled with the idea of his baby sister getting together with a biker, but once he'd returned stateside after a deployment and seen how I was with Courtney, he'd come around. After punching me in the jaw for marrying her while he was gone—the only hit I'd ever willingly let a man get in on me since I understood where he was coming from and appreciated how protective he was of her.

"Hey, big bro." Courtney shifted her arms so that her brother could get a better look at our son. "Meet Arlen Pierce Driscoll, named after two of the men most important to Pax and me. You both stepped in when each of us needed someone, and we really appreciate it."

When we found out we were having a boy, I immediately agreed to how she wanted to name him. I hadn't gotten the chance to get to know my brother-in-law very well, but I respected the fuck out of him. More because he'd done a hell of a good job looking after my girl before I came into her life than the fact that he was a Navy SEAL.

Arlen looked stunned as he asked, "You named your son after me?"

Courtney patted his hand. "He's got big shoes to fill, but I'm sure he'll live up to them with his dad, uncle, and all of the guys around to show him what's what."

"Fucking hell," he muttered, stroking a finger down the baby's cheek. "You don't know what that means to me, sis."

"Not as much as everything you've done for me since Mom and Dad passed away and growing up," she replied, sniffling.

She managed to hold back her tears during that

talk, but she lost the battle when we repeated it later that day and had the same conversation with Pierce. For some reason, it was easier for her to handle the gratitude she felt for her brother than the appreciation she had for the man who changed my life.

EPILOGUE
COURTNEY

I was living a life I never would have thought possible before I met Pax. My sexy biker was as good to me now, years later, as he had been back then. And he was such a good dad that I sometimes found myself wanting to pop out babies to give him more children to spoil. But then one of our kids would do something to drive me up the wall and make me rethink that plan.

Like right now, with our eight-year-old-son, Arlen, who I heard all the way from the front of the clubhouse, screaming his little head off.

The rest of the old ladies' eyes bugged out as I bolted around the building, only to find my eldest child and husband on the clubhouse roof, both of them with some sort of harness tied around their waists.

"What the heck is going on?" I yelled, hands on my hips as I looked up at them.

"Hey, baby." He beamed a smile at me, but it did nothing to soften my anger. Recognizing the look on my face, he decided to see if Arlen had better luck. "Son, why don't you tell her what we're doing?"

"Hi, Mom! We're rappelling," he whistled through his missing front teeth.

"Rappelling?" I echoed, raising an eyebrow.

"Yeah, let's show her, Arlen," Pax replied, squeezing our son's shoulder.

Arlen fist-bumped him before my heart leaped in my chest as they basically jumped backward off the roof, their feet landing almost in unison against the side of the building. I didn't breathe again until they were both on the ground.

"We need to do that again," Arlen cheered.

"Why don't you go play with the other kids while I talk to your dad?" I grumbled, keeping my glare on Pax.

"Aw, man," Arlen groaned before unhooking all the equipment from himself. Then he ran toward the area where one of the guys had built a playset, where some of the other kids were already playing.

Pax took a step forward, the grin still on his face. "I was right there with him, baby. You didn't need to worry."

"Then why did I hear him screaming his head off all the way from the front of the clubhouse?" I demanded.

Pax laughed. "Screaming with excitement. He was rooting around and found some of my old equipment, and I decided if he wanted to use it, I'd better teach him how to do it safely before he got any bright ideas that ended up with us racing to the emergency room."

I let my shoulders fall, my heartbeat somewhat returning to normal. "I guess it's good to be safe, but I really wished you would've warned me first. I swear, my heart almost stopped beating in my chest when I heard him scream."

"I'm sorry, baby. The last thing I wanted to do was scare you." He stripped out of his equipment, letting it fall to the ground at his feet. "Don't be mad at me."

"I can if I wanna," I pouted.

He took a step closer, his eyes going to half-mast. "How about working some of that anger off with me in private, then?"

"Pax." I moved my hand to shove his shoulder,

but he was much faster, gripping my hips and throwing me over his shoulder before I could do anything to stop him.

I couldn't help the giggle escaping my throat as the other guys laughed around us. I ignored them, my heart now pounding even faster as he headed to the room that he rarely used anymore, carrying me as though I weighed nothing until we were there.

We had our own house on the compound—something King insisted upon since Pax was his second in command, and I'd become Stella's best friend.

It looked so different and less intimidating than when I first saw it, and I felt none of the fear that I had back then when he dumped me on the same mattress.

"Arlen is going to wonder where we wandered off to," I managed to gasp.

"Then we'd better make this quick," he growled, pulling me closer to him and lifting my legs to his chest.

My earlier anger had already turned to passion, so I didn't protest when his fingers reached my damp panties underneath my sundress.

"Love how you're always so ready for me," he murmured.

"Are you going to keep talking or are you going to

give me enough orgasms to make me forget how much you just scared me?" I asked.

He laughed, unsheathing his dick and letting his pants and boxers fall to his ankles.

With one quick thrust, he had my panties pushed aside, his thick dick filling me to the hilt.

"That better?" he asked with a grunt.

"Just don't rip my panties like you did my shirt."

He groaned. "That was eight years ago, and I've bought you plenty of them since."

"Then you can buy me more panties, too," I teased.

"I'll buy you anything you want, baby," he promised with another rough thrust.

I gripped his sides as he hammered in and out of me, my orgasm boiling low in my belly.

"That's it, baby, I can feel you squeezing the life out of my cock. Come for me, now."

He punctuated his demand with a brush of his thumb over my sensitive clit. I came hard and fast, biting down on my bottom lip so I wouldn't scream out his name and risk anyone coming to check on us.

He followed soon after, his body stiffening as he spilled into me.

We both panted as he set my legs down, putting my underwear back in place.

"Are you less angry now?" he asked, helping me to my feet as he put an arm around my waist.

"Maybe a little."

He laughed, kissing my forehead. "I'll take that."

Want to know about Echo's mystery woman? Find out in Echo!

Curious about the DeLucas? Check out The Mafia Boss's Nanny!

And if you join our newsletter, you'll get an email from us with a link to claim a FREE copy of The Virgin's Guardian, which was banned on Amazon.

ABOUT THE AUTHOR

The writing duo of Elle Christensen and Rochelle Paige team up under the Fiona Davenport pen name to bring you sexy, insta-love stories filled with alpha males. If you want a quick & dirty read with a guaranteed happily ever after, then give Fiona Davenport a try!

Printed in Great Britain
by Amazon